DEVIL'S DEN

A Novella in The Johnson & Wilde Series

Andy Griffee

Copyright © 2023 Andy Griffee

All Rights Reserved

The right of Andy Griffee to be identified as the Author of the Work has been asserted by him in accordance with the Copyright, Designs and Patents Act of 1988.

All rights reserved. No part of this publication may be reproduced, stored in a retrieval system or transmitted, in any form or by any means, electronic, mechanical, photocopying, recording or otherwise, without the prior written permission of the author.

To all of my former BBC colleagues

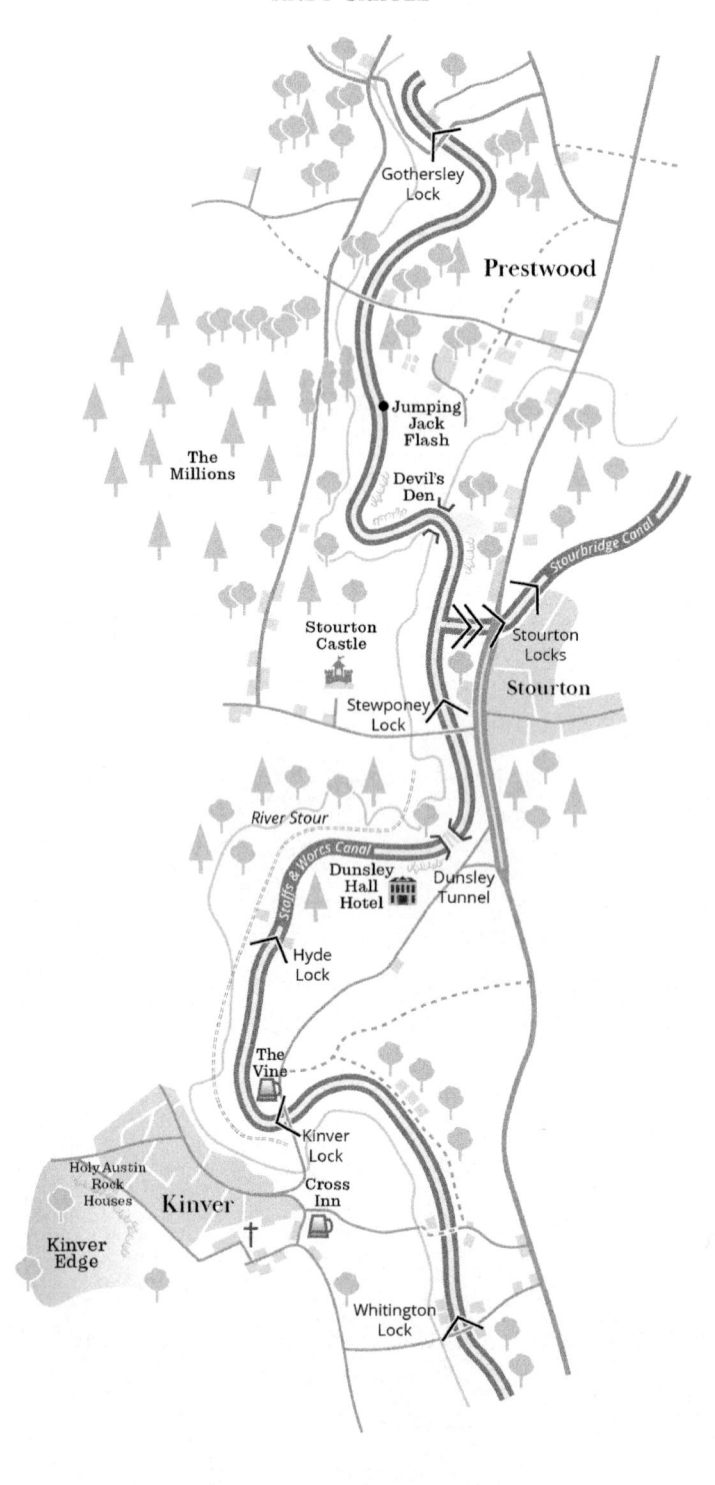

ANDY GRIFFEE

Gothersley Lock

Prestwood

Jumping Jack Flash

The Millions

Devil's Den

Stourbridge Canal

Stourton Castle

Stourton Locks

Stourton

Stewponey Lock

River Stour

Staffs & Worcs Canal

Dunsley Hall Hotel

Dunsley Tunnel

Hyde Lock

The Vine

Kinver Lock

Holy Austin Rock Houses

Kinver

Cross Inn

Kinver Edge

Whitington Lock

1

We'd come on shift at eight o'clock having cycled from our digs at Kinver through the quiet and frosty country lanes. I can still picture the steam coming in short sharp bursts from our mouths as we pedalled hard, side by side, determined not to be late and marked down in the foreman's book. Most of the other lads were living in temporary dormitories near the tunnels and work had already begun on a big new hostel above ground. We preferred our lodgings in a widow's spare bedroom in Kinver, where there was a bit of life.

Me and Jack had been digging out the Millionaire Tunnels for the past six months. We'd been transferred there from a coal pit in Nottingham to help with the war effort. The big plan in the foreman's office showed the eventual layout of the aircraft parts factory that we were tunnelling out of the earth. It revealed there would be about three and half miles of tunnels in a grid pattern with four main tunnels running east to west, high and wide enough to let big lorries travel along their length and criss-crossed with a multitude of smaller linking tunnels running north to south.

It was hard work, but better than being down the mine. Hollowing out these sandstone hills was clean work compared to bringing up coal. But that didn't mean it was any safer. We'd already lost Harry Depper and his two mates last year, in October of '41. They'd been blasting with gelignite in Tunnel One when the roof came down without any warning. All three of them had been crushed to death by the falling rock. But it was still safer than going into uniform and being shot at or torpedoed by

Jerry. I'd felt guilty at first, what with mining being a 'reserved occupation', and there were still times when someone would mutter something nasty when you were queuing for a pint at The Cross on Church Hill. But most of the locals knew we were doing our bit and taking risks for it too. And with more than a thousand men on site, we were hardly on our own, were we?

There was a rumour doing the rounds that the suits had cocked things up and that the main tunnels lost their shape when we started blasting the entrances to the linking tunnels. The lads reckoned this made the whole thing unstable – which it couldn't be if it was to survive German bombs. It was the raids on Birmingham and Coventry that had prompted the government to order the tunnels in the first place. Anyway, Sir Alex said we had to cut the smaller tunnel gallery entrances by hand instead, and Jack and I had been transferred to this new duty.

It was bloody tiring work. The pneumatic chisels were heavy and awkward, so we worked in pairs, taking it in turn to cut into the rockface and remove the spoil out of our immediate workspace. It was dark, damp and hellishly noisy what with the blasting, the chiselling and the non-stop clank, clank, clank of the conveyor belts they'd installed to remove the loose stone and boulders. We could barely hear each other until the hooter sounded for dinner and all the machinery was switched off for thirty minutes while we sat on the cold floor and munched on our spam and boiled egg sandwiches.

Jack had teased me that day. He knew I was sweet on a barmaid at The Cross called Elizabeth Shaw. Lizzy had a lovely round face, big brown eyes, a rosebud mouth and a knockout figure. Her dad was the pub's landlord and kept a close eye on her, but we'd managed to meet up at the pictures a couple of times and got along famously. The second time, she held my hand as soon as the lights went out. She was a lovely girl, kind, gentle and when she laughed two dimples appeared in the peachy soft skin of her cheeks. Jack had been with me the previous evening when she had brought two pints of Black Country ale to our table. I saw her wink as she carefully replaced my cardboard beer mat with a new one. I turned it over as soon as she returned to the bar. She had written on it in pencil. 'Tomorrow, half past seven, The Vine.'

The Vine was another of Kinver's pubs, located down by the canal and alongside Kinver Lock. Lizzy had obviously negotiated the evening off, but we'd need to be careful that none of her dad's friends spotted us together in the town's rival boozer. Jack snatched the mat off me, read the message and snorted with laughter.

"Ay up," he said. "Gilbert Shaw's a lucky boy then, ain't he? Arr, that he is. Be a mate will you and ask if she's got a friend." He winked at me. "P'raps I could come along too?"

"You're bloody joking, aren't you?" I snapped back in a whispered voice.

He chuckled and cast a glance up at the bar where the imposing pot-bellied frame of Lizzy's dad was polishing brandy glasses with a tea-towel. "So how far d'you think she'll let you go then?"

I snatched the piece of cardboard back off him. "Shut your dirty mouth, will you?" I hissed at him. "You'll ruin it with your big gob and your dirty mind. And anyway, she's a nice lass."

"Aye," he said taking a big swallow of his chestnut-coloured ale. "A nice lass with a nice …" He didn't get a chance to finish the sentence as I stretched out a hand and tipped the bottom of his glass forward so that beer spilt down the front of his shirt and tie. "What the … what did you do that for?" he spluttered.

"You know damn well," I said. "Come on. Drink up. I want my tea."

Jack returned to the topic in our dinner break the following day. We were sipping our brew out of metal flasks after finishing our grub. "So then, all excited about tonight then, are we?"

"Aye, it should be fun. We'll need to get away sharpish," I replied. "I want to get back in plenty of time for a wash and change."

"There's talk of overtime on offer. They want this place up and running as soon as possible. Apparently, there's a war on."

I nodded and finished off my tea. "Can't blame them," I said. "There were a lot of planes heading for Brum last night." We had both turned out the light, opened the blackout curtains and leaned on our shared bedroom window to watch the searchlights on the horizon and listen to the far-off explosions of another bombing raid on the big manufacturing cities of the Midlands. "But bugger overtime. I'm seeing Lizzy tonight and neither the foreman nor Adolf are going to stop me."

We worked on through the afternoon with me checking my pocket watch regularly in the dust-filled gloom. The monotonous vibration of the chisel combined with my anticipation of seeing Lizzy made me careless and I found Jack taking his turn at the face more and more frequently. Finally, at last, the hooter sounded to signal the end of the shift. We had been working at the far western end of the complex which would mean a long walk back along Tunnel Three to its entrance after we had stored the chisel away. The main tunnel had a cable looping along its high roof with lights suspended at regular intervals above the conveyor belt. The belt took debris out into the open where it was transferred into lorries by dumper trucks. Unusually, the conveyor belt had not been switched off this time, although the last of the day's spoil had disappeared along its length and out into the open air. Small groups of workmen were already walking alongside the clanking machinery, grateful that another day of hard physical graft had come to an end. I smelt a whiff of cigarette smoke. Someone had already lit-up a crafty woodbine – which was against the rules. I smiled to myself. In another hour I would be holding Lizzy's hand in a dark corner of The Vine and enjoying a pint and a proper roll-up myself.

It would take ten to fifteen minutes to leave the main tunnel and clock-off and another twenty minutes to cycle to our digs. That would leave precious little time for me to stand in a metal tub, wipe off the day's dirt and grime and change into something respectable. What if I was late and Lizzy gave up on me? I peered anxiously along the main tunnel which was just over half a mile long. A lot of other lads were dawdling along its length and blocking the way. I couldn't break into a run even if I wanted to. I looked at the conveyor belt trundling past me. It was still going much faster than a walking pace.

"Jack," I shouted above its noise. I remember grinning at him as I looped one strap of my knapsack through one arm. "I'm in a hurry. C'mon. Let's take a ride!" I put one hand on the steel safety bar and vaulted into the centre of the moving belt.

Then I crouched down on all fours and looked behind me. Jack had done the same and was laughing as he sat on his backside and bumped along. We started to overtake the other miners and they began to laugh and cheer as they realised what we were doing. Jack had both hands raised in triumph and he was shouting something I couldn't hear as we continued to be carried past the other lads. I was kneeling up now, caught up in the moment and acknowledging their cheers in the same way as Jack. One part of me knew we'd get a right dressing down if a foreman saw us, but the other part of me was determined not to be late for Lizzy - and I was enjoying the attention. I was going to be a legend.

On we went, closer and closer to the main tunnel's entrance. I could sense the fresh air rushing towards us and I could still hear the cheering above the noise of the conveyor belt's machinery and its squealing rollers. No-one had ever done this before. The belt was usually switched off as soon as the end-of-shift hooter sounded. And that's when it happened.

I had one hand raised in triumph and I had just dropped it when my knapsack slipped down the length of my arm. The strap on the other side flicked sideways across my back. The buckle must have worked itself loose. The strap wrapped itself around the end of one of the steel tubes which were carrying the belt. It was over in seconds. I was powerless as the knapsack yanked my head down sideways and towards the jaws of the remorseless machinery. The last thing I saw was Jack, hurtling closer to me, his mouth open in horror and his arms outstretched in front of him as he tried to fend off the inevitable collision.

CHAPTER 1

The Devil's Den! I just couldn't resist it. My Pearson's Canal Companion showed that the intriguingly named location came just after an aqueduct and just before a sharp bend on the Staffs & Worcs Canal. I had first seen it as my finger traced our route northwards after leaving the mighty River Severn at Stourport. The little book said The Devil's Den was the location of a peculiar cave cut out of the rocks and which was thought to have been used as a boathouse by the Foley family of Prestwood Hall. It was a tiny detail on our future journey, but it stuck in my mind, and I was looking forward to seeing this mysteriously named feature.

"Typical," laughed Nina, my occasional crewmate and companion on Jumping Jack Flash, the 64 ft long narrowboat I call my home. "Trust you to get all excited about somewhere called Devil's Den. It'll just be a hole carved in some rock. What are you expecting? A midnight witches' coven on the towpath?"

Nina was no longer living in Oxford and had spent much of the last nine months cruising England's canals and rivers with me and Eddie, my lively little border-terrier. However, her elderly mother had become ill during the summer and she had been forced to make increasingly regular detours back to the family home to organise carers, district nurses and GP appointments. Another departure was imminent and so I was planning to moor up until she could re-join me.

There is never any question of me accompanying her on these trips home as I am persona non grata to her family and friends. They still blame yours truly for helping her to go missing after the death in combat of her army officer husband. They raised a collective eyebrow at her 'bizarre' decision to share my 'alternative lifestyle' as a narrowboat liveaboard. And they had read my newspaper articles and books about our tangles with the Midlands Canal Pusher and Russian gangsters in Bath with increasing alarm. There had been no book about our most recent adventure in Oxford, but the experience had been both a blessing and a curse. It had left my bank balance in a much healthier state and with no requirement for paid journalistic employment, at least for the time being, we had been able to cruise the canal network as we wished.

But Oxford had also been a painful hiccup in our burgeoning relationship and our current status could be described as unromantic and platonic – definitely 'friends without benefits'. Nevertheless, we had been through a lot together, we enjoyed our canalboat lifestyle and we both had a deep and enduring affection for the little brown dog who shared my boat. And I still harboured the passionate hope that one day Nina would overcome her grief for her dead husband and find herself able to love me as much as I loved her.

We had not lingered in Stourport for very long. The town owes its very existence to the canal trade and it had some interesting features around its basins – especially the vast bulk of the Tontine Hotel – a hundred-bedroom riverside establishment that had been converted into homes. But we hurried on through the little town. It felt like a landlocked seaside resort with its brash amusement arcades, noisy riverside funfair, junk food outlets and shops selling kiss-me-quick hats. I had popped into the High Street to collect some cash and watched in fascination as five large men on mobility scooters arrived in a convoy, parked outside a pub and unsteadily decanted themselves into it. Closed and empty shops stretched along the street on both sides, like missing teeth in a decaying mouth.

The next town, Kidderminster, wasn't much better. The rich heritage of its world famous carpet industry had given way to more fast-food businesses, charity shops, supermarkets and retail parks - all surrounded by busy ring-roads. The smell of fried onion hung heavy in the air and we moved on after just one night on a mooring surrounded by redundant carpet mills, empty warehouses and the constant hum of traffic that left us sleep deprived.

However, the countryside opened up after Cookley Tunnel and became truly lovely as we approached the little town of Kinver. I had read all about Kinver Edge, a wooded ridge rising to 500 ft which I reckoned would suit Eddie just fine for some long autumnal walks. But I hadn't reckoned on the loveliness of our route as we puttered on at three miles per hour through the Stour Valley. Trees spilled down to the towpath – both deciduous and conifers. At times they would give way to sweeping meadows or occasional small cliffs or outcrops made of the smooth red sandstone that characterised the area. The little river Stour could be glimpsed running alongside the towpath, parallel with the canal.

"This is quite lovely," said Nina as she sat near me at the tiller with Eddie on her lap. "It's so peaceful – and unexpected."

I nodded and checked our location again on Pearson's little landscape map. We were approaching Stewponey Lock where Nina would hop off Jumping Jack Flash to prepare the water level and open the gates.

"And yet, it must have been complete chaos along here when there were twenty puddling furnaces producing wrought iron to be shipped away. You just can't imagine it now, can you?"

Nina had taken the map from me to study it for herself. "Not far till Devil's Den then," she observed with a grin. "Are you excited?"

I shrugged. "Just intrigued. "Now then, are you going to earn your keep and open that lock?" I had been keeping a close eye on the Canal and River Trust's towpath signs which indicate maximum mooring durations for continuous cruisers like us. The permanent moorings immediately after Kinver had given way to 2-day and 5-day posts but I knew, as soon as they stopped, I could stay for up to two weeks without being told to move on. That should give Nina plenty of time to travel down to her mother's home in Wiltshire and back.

The last 5-day mooring post appeared just after the canal widened out into its picturesque junction with the Stourbridge Canal. A narrowboat was tied up at Stourton Junction with a large triangular clothes horse unfolded on its bow. Rows and rows of socks and pants hung limply in the damp and windless September air. As we passed, we could look up at the first flight of four locks climbing up for the start of the Stourbridge Canal's route towards the Birmingham Canal Navigations and the rest of the Black Country. There was no sign of anyone on board the moored boat, but the nature of the generously sized his-and-her underpants suggested that it belonged to a middle-aged couple. It made me wonder what kind of speculation our own boat caused. No doubt people automatically assumed that we were a couple – an impression reinforced by the presence of Eddie. I sighed heavily. One day, maybe, one day.

Woodland spilled down on every side of the junction as we headed onwards. An attractive white signpost told us we were heading towards the metropolis of Wolverhampton. Then the canal suddenly swung left after we passed a small entrance into a large round pool of water. We had arrived at the little aqueduct just before The Devil's Den. We could glimpse the Stour meandering below the curved bricks that topped the walls flanking the bridge. It was an idyllic spot.

"Look," said Nina moments later, "There it is."

I followed her pointed finger and saw a small cliff of red sandstone largely obscured by green ivy and other vegetation that cascaded down from the trees above it. There was a black arched wooden door at the level of the water. This must be the entrance to The Devil's Den. It too was partly obscured by greenery and we might easily have missed it if we hadn't been primed in advance by our route map. I slipped the engine into reverse to stall our progress and stared at the door. "Could it open out into a boathouse on the other side do you think?"

"It would be a pretty small boat, wouldn't it?" said Nina. "You certainly couldn't get a narrowboat through that entrance. Perhaps it was for some kind of rowing skiff for the gentry to play around on?"

"And yet, it's such a strange name – The Devil's Den. Why would you call a boathouse that? Surely there must have been a reason for it?"

We swung sharply right onto a fairly long straight stretch of the canal. The towpath on our left still sloped away towards the Stour and fields, but the right-hand bank was steep sided and topped with trees. I could hear the traffic on a road above and beyond them. At one point, the bank suddenly opened out. A rectangle had been cut out of the cliff for some reason creating a kind of watery layby that was approximately the length of my boat. I could see a road bridge crossing the canal up ahead.

"This'll do," I said firmly. "My home for the next fortnight – or at least until you come back from mummy." I eased over to the towpath opposite the little cutting and silenced the engine. It took less than five minutes to drive two heavy duty mooring stakes into the ground at the bow and stern and secure the mooring ropes. Nina had the kettle boiling as I climbed back on board. "It's a nice quiet spot," I said. "But I can easily cycle back into Kinver for provisions …"

"… and a pub," interrupted Nina.

"Your constant commentary on my modest alcohol intake is becoming quite tiresome."

"Tea?" she asked pointedly.

"I might have a whisky," I declared stubbornly. The light outside was fading fast and it was getting chilly, but the boat would quickly warm up once I had the little multifuel stove going.

"You'll have tea," she said.

I had tea.

CHAPTER 2

Later that evening, after a reheated chicken casserole and a blackberry and apple crumble made with fruit from the canal's hedgerows, I persuaded Nina that Eddie needed a decent stretch of his legs and that it might as well be in the direction of a welcoming hostelry. So, we ambled back the way we had come with Eddie off his leash and happily leading the way in the light from our two powerful torches.

The ever-helpful Pearson's guide had listed the Cross Inn at Kinver as a CAMRA prize winner which repaid the climb up Church Hill, and so that is where we headed. I remembered the church looking down on us from its rocky outcrop as we motored towards the little town. We opened the pub door on a crowded and lively scene. It appeared that a Monday night pub quiz had just finished and all the tables were taken, so we squeezed into a space at the bar and ordered a pint and a half of a Black Country Ale. It was called Pig on the Wall for some reason.

"Have you ordered a taxi for the morning?" I yelled into Nina's ear. The din meant I had to lean in close to her head, which wasn't too much of a hardship. I enjoyed a moment's inhalation of the familiar apple-scent of her shampoo before returning to my chestnut-brown beer.

"Yep," she nodded. "It's going to park by that road bridge up ahead of our mooring and I'll be off by 9 o'clock. The train goes at 10, so that leaves plenty of time."

I nodded to save myself the trouble of trying to be heard above the surrounding hubbub. Perhaps we should have stayed on the boat and had a quiet night in? Eddie was being very well behaved;

admittedly, he gets a lot of practice at lying patiently under pub tables, but I was worried someone might tread on him in the crush.

"Ooh look. Come on, quick" said Nina suddenly. She was off and away from the bar, making rapid progress towards a corner table where four members of a quiz team were standing to put on their coats. I pulled Eddie to his feet and trailed in her wake through the scrum. However, another younger couple had the same idea and arrived at the table at the same time as Nina.

"Why don't we share?" Nina was asking as I joined her.

"Sure, no problem," smiled the other woman, and we all claimed our seats with a sense of relief.

"Busy in here tonight," said the younger man to the woman. "But it always is on a Monday with the quiz." He looked to be in his mid-twenties and was clean-shaven with good teeth and thick black wavy hair. His dark suit, black tie and white shirt were unnaturally smart for a beer pub. I wondered if he had been to a funeral. His aftershave smelt cheap and strong.

"I'm Heloise. Hel for short. And this is Nick," said the young woman. Nick nodded without much enthusiasm. I guessed they were on a date and he didn't want any rival distractions. I pointed at my crewmate. "This is Nina, I'm Jack … and this is Eddie," I said as the little dog's head appeared from below to see what was going on.

"Oh, he's lovely," cooed Heloise. "He looks like a teddy bear."

"He's like one of those meerkats in the adverts," said Nick without a smile.

Heloise reached across to fondle one of Eddie's triangular ear flaps. She looked the same sort of age as Nick but, in contrast to his darkness, her hair had been dyed white which looked strangely old above her pretty, freckled young face. He had a strong square jaw which also contrasted with her elfin chin and his sober attire contrasted strangely with her bohemian appearance. She wore ochre-coloured dungarees with a bib and braces above a green fisherman's jumper. Loops of coloured beads hung around her neck. But it was her eyes which caught my attention. They were a pure and startlingly intense sapphire blue. Could they be contact lenses? I didn't think so. I remembered a recent magazine article about the actor Paul Newman who wore dark glasses all the time because he was constantly being pestered by fans to show them his eyes. They must have been identical to this girl. Nick caught me staring and gave a little snort of irritation.

"Anyway Hel," he said, dragging his friend's attention away from Eddie, "I was telling you about the silver delivery." Heloise shrugged apologetically at us. It was clear that Nick didn't want to waste time talking to a couple of strangers. The couple turned inwards on each other to continue their conversation and Nina and I did likewise. The only problem was, he had instantly caught my interest when he mentioned the 'silver delivery'.

Experienced television and radio presenters develop an ability to speak perfect sentences to their audience whilst simultaneously taking in the instructions from a director or a producer or gallery assistant in their earpiece. This gives them an enviable social skill. It means they can hold a convincing conversation with one person at a party, while scanning the room at the same time to pick up something more interesting - or even to overhear what is being said about them. Sadly, I do not have this ability, but Nina quickly realised that I was trying to listen to Nick rather than to her. Fortunately, Nick's reference to the 'silver delivery' had also piqued her curiosity and so we both relaxed into making desultory noises at each other as we tuned into the conversation of our table companions.

"It was amazing Hel, honestly amazing. This convoy of trucks turned up with armed guards and everything and the lads unloaded nearly two and a half thousand bars of the stuff. They reckon it weighed sixty tonnes in total."

"Blimey," she said. "How much is that worth?'

Nick raised three fingers at her and then folded one so there were only two left outstretched. "Thirty – two – million – pounds," he said slowly before laughing and taking a long swig of his beer. "Can you believe it? And all of it just lying in a wreck at the bottom of the Indian Ocean for years and years until this guy found it. Bloody incredible."

"So how come it's in the tunnels?" asked Heloise.

"Well, it's not his yet, is it? At least I don't think it is. Some court has to decide if it's proper salvage – so it's being stored by us until there's a judge's ruling or something. Quite a thing really," he added. "Anyway, keep it to yourself." I sensed him glancing across the table to where Nina and I were turned in on each other but listening intently. "Although, I bet if you could read the guy's cards, you could tell him whether he gets to keep the dosh or not! And maybe he'd give you a cut. That would be nice, wouldn't it? You could fix up your boat." They both laughed at that. Their conversation moved on to discuss a film they had seen recently while Nina and I chatted about her mum's health problems and the progress of her beloved niece, Anna, who is a student at Oxford university.

Nick stood up after about fifteen minutes. "I need a slash. D'you want another drink?"

"No thanks," Heloise replied. "You can walk me back in a bit."

The young woman went back to petting Eddie as soon as her friend had departed for the gents. I was desperate to find out more about the silver-salvage story. What were these tunnels he had mentioned? On reflection, his dark suit and white shirt could be the uniform of some kind of security guard. That would make sense. It all sounded like the makings of a bloody good story and one that I could easily sell to the national press. But how could I admit to listening-in to their conversation? And anyway, it seemed as though it was Nick who knew all the facts rather than the exotic-looking Heloise. Not for the first time, it was Nina who came to my rescue.

"I'm sorry Heloise," she said politely across the table. "You have such a lovely name by the way. I couldn't help hearing your friend say that you read the cards. Would that be tarot cards by any chance? I'm fascinated by that kind of thing." I looked at Nina quizzically. I had never heard Nina express any kind of interest in fortune telling. Heloise nodded her head enthusiastically. Oh God, I thought to myself, here we go – cue a lot of ridiculous mumbo-jumbo aimed at parting the credulous from their cash.

"Thank you. I had a French mother - but please call me Hel. All my friends do. Yes, I'm a professional reader," she said with a wide-open smile. "I've done courses and everything. My mum always said I had the gift and it turned out I did! Have you ever had your cards read?"

"Um no, I haven't," admitted Nina.

"Oh, you should! I'll give you a special price if you like. It's not scary or anything. We can do it on my boat."

"You live on a narrowboat?" said Nina.

"Yeah, worse blooming luck. It's falling apart and I need to spend some money to get me through the winter."

"Jack lives on a narrowboat too. We've just moored up beyond Stourton Junction. It's called Jumping Jack Flash."

"Ah that's nice!" she exclaimed cheerfully. "We're nearly neighbours then. I've got one of the permanent moorings just beyond The Vine. My uncle gave it to me. He died last year." The Vine is another of Kinver's pubs next to a canal lock which we had passed through earlier in the day. "My boat's called Magic Meg. Why don't you come over tomorrow afternoon and we'll have a reading?"

"Nina's got to catch a train first thing in the morning," I explained apologetically.

"Oh, that's a shame."

"My mum is quite poorly. I have to go and see her," explained Nina.

Hel's amazing eyes drooped in sympathy and she reached out to cover Nina's hand on the table. No-one said anything for about thirty seconds. Then she withdrew her hand and smiled sadly at Nina, as though she knew something but didn't want to say it. I dismissed the gesture as amateur theatrics.

"But maybe Jack could have his cards read?" Nina said suddenly.

My head snapped round at her. "What?"

"That's a great idea!" said Hel. "Although Nick likes to be on the boat if I read cards for any other men."

"That's fine. That's perfect," said Nina.

"Now hang on a minute …"

"Shall we say 6 o'clock? He'll be off shift by then."

And then it hit me. If Nick was going to be there, I might learn more about the delivery of the silver bars from the seabed worth £32 million. Somehow, Nina had manoeuvred me into an opportunity to find out more details – maybe enough to make a sellable story. And in the meantime, I could do a bit more online research. "Uh yes, okay. Let's say six o'clock at Mystic Meg then."

"Magic Meg," corrected Nina.

"I'm sorry. Magic Meg."

"Lovely," said Heloise, standing to hand a coat to the returning Nick. "It'll be £50 for the reading. Cash only please."

Nick was smiling. "I can't leave you for five seconds, can I?" He turned to look at Nina. "Sold you a card reading, has she?"

"No, Nina's got to visit her mum tomorrow," said Heloise. "I'm reading Jack's cards at six o'clock after you get off work. That's alright, isn't it?"

Nick looked distinctly annoyed that the reading was for me rather than Nina. "It'll have to be, won't it," he said tersely. "Right, we're off." He nodded at me. "See you tomorrow. Don't forget, it's cash only."

"We should go too. This beer's quite strong and I don't want another," said Nina.

We trailed behind the young couple at a discreet distance before they turned off the towpath and stepped across onto a down-at-heel boat with a lot of plant pots ranged untidily along its peeling roof.

"Yes, well, thanks for that," I said grumpily to Nina after we'd passed by their closing hatchway.

She linked her arm in mine and laughed. "I can read you like a book, Jack Johnson. You were desperate to get that story about the silver and now you've got a chance to find out more. You should be thanking me rather than whinging about it."

"But bloody tarot cards!" I protested. "And fifty quid too."

She tightened her arm in mine. "Stop moaning. It'll give you something to do while I'm away and you'll earn a lot more than £50 if you can sell the story. Besides, you might learn something about yourself that you didn't know. I think there's something in it. And you know what they say don't you?"

"What?"

She pressed her palms together in mock meditation. "Those who are enlightened never stop forging themselves."

"Oh, yes? And you know what else they say don't you?"

"What?"

"Oh, something about how terribly hard it is to be the only one who knows the truth!"

"Well, you don't need to worry about that do you Jack?" said Nina, unhooking her arm as we reached Jumping Jack Flash and clicking her finger for Eddie to follow her across our little boarding plank. "Because I know the truth, the whole truth and nothing but the truth about you, don't I?" She unlocked the doors, pushed them backwards, slid back the hatchway cover and went inside chuckling to herself while I tried to puzzle out what she meant by that.

CHAPTER 3

Jumping Jack Flash has two single berths opposite each other and immediately after the stern steps. When Nina is on board, Eddie sleeps on one of them while she sleeps in the other. When Nina isn't on board, Eddie condescends to sleep on the floor alongside my double berth bed, which is in the centre of the boat.

I was woken the next morning by the noises of both of them moving about. My mobile phone told me it was 7.30 a.m. and I blearily started scanning the BBC News website to see if anything had happened overnight. It was chilly on-board, and condensation misted the glass of the small circular portholes above my bed and on the opposite wall. However, I could still make out Nina's lycra-clad calves and green trainers as she jogged past with Eddie alongside her. I knew I would have about half-an-hour before she returned from their morning run for a hot drink and a shower. I snuggled down for an extra ten-minutes and brought up the search app on my phone.

It took just seconds for 'silver salvage £32m' to bring up a whole list of press stories. So much for me being able to sell the story - it was already out there and everywhere. I pulled up an article from The Times. It described how a 69-year-old British treasure hunter had organised a secret expedition to rescue 2,364 bars of silver from the wreck of the SS Tilawa. The ship had been torpedoed by a Japanese submarine in 1942, 930 miles north-east of the Seychelles. The Tilawa stayed afloat before being struck by a second torpedo and 281 passengers and crew had been lost. The treasure hunter was called Ross Hyett. He also dabbled in a bit of racing driving and had set up a company to locate shipwrecks at previously unexplored depths.

However, after learning of the find, the South African government had claimed 'sovereign' rights over the silver because it had been en-route from Bombay to the country's mint at the time. The recovered ingots had already been shipped to Southampton docks and were now thought to be in a secret and secure storage unit until a High Court judge could rule on the claim. A 'secret and secure storage unit' which I now knew something about. Or did I? All I knew was that our friend Nick had mentioned tunnels of some kind. I was about to start searching the internet for a tunnel complex close to Kinver when I heard the stern doors banging. Nina quickly appeared through the swing door which separated our sleeping quarters.

Her face was flushed and there were beads of sweat on her brow. Her hair was swept back into a short ponytail. "Hey you! Why isn't the kettle on, you slacker?"

"Oops. Sorry. Caught red-handed. Have your shower first and I'm on it."

"No. That's not the order of doing things." You can see why I refer to her as the head-girl. Tutting audibly, she moved on past my bed into the galley and began banging about with the kettle and the gas ring. Chastened, I swung my legs onto the deck and padded off to the loo in my boxer shorts and T-shirt.

Nina was pouring boiling water into a teapot on the little table between the galley and the bow as I returned. I yanked on a dressing gown and joined her. "Good run?" I ventured, keen to make-up for my indiscipline and send her off to her mum in a better mood.

"It's a lovely spot," she conceded. "Although, there's a hornet's nest in the hollow of a tree just past the tunnel. You need to make sure Eddie doesn't stick his nose in there."

"Understood. Thanks," I said. "I'm sorry about the tea. I was caught up in some stories about that silver delivery." I told her what I had learned and found The Times article again for her to study while we sipped our Earl Grey.

"So, the 'secret' location of the silver isn't quite so secret now that Jack Johnson, the famous reporter knows all about it," she commented.

"Well, it is really. Nick mentioned some tunnels, but I don't really know anything more than that."

"But they must be local to here," she said thoughtfully. "Maybe you can find out more this evening – when you're having your future told."

I curled one side of my top lip in disgust. "Yes, I'm not looking forward to that. And anyway, I'm not sure that revealing the current location of the silver is much of a story now it's all out there. That reminds me, I haven't got much cash left. Can you lend me any?"

She shook her head firmly. "You can take Eddie into town and find a cashpoint after I've gone. You'll need £50. And stop sulking. You can afford it."

It's true, my bank balance was much healthier than it had been for a long time thanks to a contract I had signed in Oxford with a rich American TV evangelist. His son had committed suicide after killing his girlfriend and the old man had insisted on contracting me to not write about it.

"Now, I need to get showered and dressed for my trip to see mummy," added Nina. Eddie cocked his head on one side, a charming characteristic of border-terriers when they are having a good think, and then trotted off after her. I knew he'd sulk for a bit when she started packing her bags, but he would be fine after the distraction of another walk later in the day.

I busied myself making poached eggs on toast with a fresh mug of tea before Nina brushed herself down, gave me a hug, gave Eddie a much longer hug and set off for her taxi. "Now don't forget, I want a full report on the tarot card reading," were her parting words. "Chapter and verse. Nothing left out. All the juicy bits." I stayed at the tiller, gloomily watching her swaying coat until she was out of sight. Eddie was sitting at my feet with my foot on his leash to prevent him chasing after Nina. He was whimpering quietly in protest. "I know, I know Edward," I said, dipping down to fondle his ears. "You and me both."

I carried out routine tasks for the rest of the morning, washing down the roof and the sides of the boat and paying special attention to the grinning image of a court jester that was painted on the port side. I always felt there was something sinister and slightly malevolent about the picture of Jumping Jack Flash. Many pedestrians on the towpath, who are known as gongoozlers, had commented on how his eyes seemed to follow them as they passed by. Nevertheless, he was an integral part of my boat and once, having painted over him in order to hide from some ne'er-do-wells in the Midlands, I had him faithfully recreated in his vivid green and red diamond patterned suit.

I ran a damp cloth across the boat's interior surfaces, cleaned the bathroom sink, shower and loo and even emptied the fridge to give it a wipe over. Eddie watched all this activity from the safe vantage point of one of the easy chairs and with a sorrowful look in his big brown eyes. Finally, I cracked. "Okay old chap, a walk it is." His chin remained resolutely resting on his front paws. Perhaps he feared he was about to swap his comfortable chair for the hard floor of a drinking establishment or perhaps he was still hoping for Nina's quick return. Eventually, he fell into step with me on the towpath and we ambled back past The Devil's Den, across the aqueduct, and past the Stourton junction, Dunsley Tunnel and the two locks that separated our mooring from Kinver. There was no sign of life on Magic Meg as we went past – although I stopped briefly to study Heloise's floating home. She was right, it looked like it needed quite a lot of tender loving care and that wouldn't be cheap.

I was tempted to explore The Vine at Kinver Lock but decided to press on and take a look at the High Street instead. I had read that Kinver was a bustling centre for tourists and hikers throughout the summer, but it was quiet on this cold autumnal day with just a small number of locals doing their shopping. Nina and I keep a couple of fold-away Brompton bicycles on the boat and both of them needed some attention – so when I saw the sign for a bicycle repair shop, I swung off the main street and down a little side alley with tiny shops on either side. Sure enough, there was a bike shop at the far end, but even better, next to it was a cosy little seating area covered by canvas stretched over a large metal frame. It had wooden pub tables and benches and a bar stood at one end under a sign promising craft-beer. A young waiter went past me with a tray of good-looking pizzas. This felt like a discovery and after sitting down and studying the menu, Eddie had no reason to disagree. There was a page at the back called Doggo Menu offering Sliced Lashford Sausages, Waggy Doggy Ice Cream and unlimited bowls of water for canine customers.

I ordered a burger and a cloudy German ale for myself and some of the dog sausages and water for my four-legged friend and began thinking about the silver story again as we waited for our food. The Times said the silver had been declared to the Receiver of Wrecks, an official who oversees salvage law. So the ingots were probably in this person's custody until legal ownership was established. And presumably he, or she, had decided these tunnels near Kinver were the safest place to keep them. The bearded barman placed my beer in front of me and shortly afterwards another closely bearded waiter appeared with our food.

"Excuse me sir, may I?" he asked, indicating the plate of sausage slices and Eddie, who was sitting up and paying full attention now.

"Just a couple," I said. The man, who looked and sounded Eastern European, bent down on one knee to feed Eddie and ruffle his neck.

"He's a nice dog. I like dogs," said the man.

"Do you live around here?" I asked.

He looked up at me warily. "Um yes. But not for very long. Why do you ask me this?"

"Oh, I was just wondering if you knew about some tunnels near here. They're used as a warehouse of some kind I think." The impact of my question was truly surprising. The man shot rapidly to his feet and pressed his hands together in front of him. His eyes were wide and fearful, and he shook his head from left to right as he stammered to get his words out.

"What? What? But why? Why do you ask me this? I know nothing of any tunnels. Nothing. Do you hear me?" He was backing away from me now, but his strange behaviour and shrill voice had attracted the attention of a couple on a neighbouring table. "I have only just come here. To this place. Please. Please leave me alone." With that, he turned on his heels and disappeared into a small brick building behind the bar. I swapped a look of total bemusement with the couple. The man had looked terrified. I was even more baffled when, minutes later, I watched him emerge from the building. He was pulling a coat on over his apron. He shot me a suspicious look before hurrying away, back down the alley towards the High Street. How strange. There was no question about it. The man had completely panicked as soon as I mentioned the tunnels.

"I'm sorry," I said to the other waiter when it came to settling my bill. "I seem to have upset your colleague but I'm not sure why." The man handed me back my debit card and gave me a cool look.

"He had to go home," he said calmly. "Some kind of domestic problem. I'm sure it was nothing to do with you."

"Oh. Okay. Right. Thanks."

"Yep thanks. Enjoy the rest of your day." And that was that. But the incident troubled me, and I couldn't get it out of my mind as we wandered back to the boat via a cashpoint machine. By the time we reached the mooring, I was determined to find out more about these mysterious and secret tunnels, by whatever means I could.

CHAPTER 4

I piled some newspaper, kindling and logs into the little stove, lit it with some fire-lighter cubes and settled Eddie into his basket with two more pieces of the Lashford sausages. Then I switched on some of the wall lamps with their gold-coloured shades. The light was beginning to darken outside. There was nowhere nicer to be than my cosy home on the water at this time of day, and at this time of year.

I had been persuaded to buy the second-hand boat from a hire company because the share from my divorce was pretty meagre and I had no desire to start trying to climb the mortgage mountain again. But I was in good company. Spiralling house prices, a shortage of homes and climbing mortgage rates meant that hundreds more people were choosing to become narrowboat liveaboards each year. An online news article had recently told me that there were more people living on England's waterways now than at any time during the height of the Industrial Revolution. It wasn't a free existence by any means. You still had to pay for an annual licence, diesel, boat maintenance and marina fees, if you got fed up with continuous cruising. And few people ever sold their boat for a profit – unlike homes made of bricks and mortar. But I had come to love my water-rat lifestyle and especially the way I could just pack up my home and leave if I grew to dislike the neighbourhood or the neighbours.

First, I unfolded two of my Ordnance Survey maps, one covering Kidderminster & Wyre Forest and the other, Birmingham & Wolverhampton. Our present mooring was on the extreme edge of both maps, so I pieced them together and folded them until they were a manageable size on my little table. After ten minutes of close study, I could see no reference to any tunnels in the immediate vicinity and so I widened my search area to the west because the east was heavily populated and covered with housing. After admitting defeat in that direction, I returned to studying the built-up areas of Wolverhampton until my eyes were itching with the effort. This was hopeless. I needed to try another way.

I fetched my Pearson's guide from its shelf near the hatchway. Yes, I thought so. My eyes had skipped over the commentary previously, but now it registered a reference to 'underground chambers, hewn out of the area's soft sandstone for the manufacture and storage of munitions during the Second World War. And even more unnervingly, it went on, "these subterranean labyrinths were earmarked as a seat of regional government in the event of a nuclear war." These had to be the tunnels Rob had briefly mentioned. Were they now being used as some kind of secret warehouse facility? But there was no name for them in Pearson's, and there was no sign of them on the little landscape maps which followed the route of the canal. Where else could I look?

I pulled out my laptop from the drawer under my bed and opened it on top of the pile of paper. I googled 'tunnels near Kinver' and groaned. I could have saved myself time and trouble because the first thing to come up was a Wikipedia entry entitled 'Millionaire Tunnels'. "The Millionaire Tunnels," it said, "are a former underground complex beneath the Millions nature reserve, north of Kidderminster and west of Wolverhampton, covering 285,000 sq ft (26,500 sq m) with a total length of around 3.5 miles (5.6 km). They were originally built as a Second World War shadow factory and were developed during the Cold War to be a fall-back government centre."

I moved the laptop sideways to consult the map again. Yes, there on the far eastern edge of the less populated map was a large expanse of green called The Millions. Its perimeter was very close to our mooring. I would work out the distance later. But strangely, there was no indication of the tunnels on the map. I put another log in the stove and began to read about their remarkable history.

Work on digging the tunnels began in July 1941, almost two years after the war started. The Ministry of Aircraft Production had ordered that the local sandstone was to be mined to create an underground factory for the Rover car company. The company was making engines for the Bristol Aeroplane Company at the time, so the new complex was to be used to supply spare parts to its overground factories and act as a back-up if they were put out of action by enemy bombs. The new underground factory was to be laid out in a grid system with four main tunnels used for access and the movement of raw materials. They would be criss-crossed with smaller tunnels to supply workshop and storage space.

I read on. Several tragic accidents took place during the construction of the tunnels, resulting in the death of six men and one woman. First of all, a roof collapsed without warning and buried three of the miners. Then a woman was hit by one of the dump trucks and later died 'of shock'. The next two deaths happened when two of the construction workers decided to ride on top of a conveyor belt that had been installed to remove the loose rock. They became tangled up in the machinery and were mangled to death. That must have been a horrible way to die. Finally, a security officer was leaving the complex on his motorbike when he was struck down by a coach used to deliver the workers each day.

Once finished, more than 3,000 people worked in the tunnels, producing aircraft parts for the war effort. They arrived in bus and truck convoys until purpose-built hostels and dormitories could be completed to save the precious petrol. Then they worked all day, from 7.30 am until 5.30 pm in tunnels with artificial light. Rover tried to ease the working conditions by installing bars, billiard rooms and games rooms near to the sickbay. They also brought in ENSA artists to give concerts.

Finally, they piped George Formby and other music over the Tannoy System. I chuckled to imagine the endless committee meetings and minutes that preceded that brave decision. No doubt the music could only just be heard over the noise of the machinery as the workforce churned out precision engineered parts for hour after hour.

After the war, The Millionaire Tunnels became a storage facility for aeroplane and tank engines. But, as the Cold War developed, it was realised that the tunnels could provide a suitable refuge for government in the event of a nuclear war. A new canteen, dormitories, a BBC studio, offices and blast proof doors were installed to protect the politicians and civil servants who would attempt to run whatever was left of the country after the Russians had dropped the atom bomb.

And then, in 1993, the government abandoned the entire complex in favour of a new purpose-built bunker under the Ministry of Defence in Whitehall. The tunnel complex was auctioned off to its present owners in 1994 for a few hundred thousand pounds. I scrolled up. I scrolled down. I re-read entire sections. But the story stopped there. There was no reference to any kind of security warehouse, just the establishment of a Preservation Trust to fight redevelopment plans and talk of creating an underground museum of some kind. How intriguing.

I trawled around the internet a bit more and found a collection of photographs of The Millionaire Tunnels. They showed long arched and square-shaped underground tunnels with pitted walls that had mostly been painted white, rooms with rusting machinery and others with low metal beds. No mattresses. There was also an exterior daylight view of an unprepossessing arched entranceway into the tunnels. It was located at the end of a rectangular ravine that had been hewn out of the rock and was now lined with vegetation. A small group of people were clustered outside it, as though waiting to go inside. Perhaps it was a tour party? Judging by their clothes, it was a recent picture.

I checked my watch. Five o'clock. Nina would tell me to wait for at least another hour, but Nina wasn't here. I poured myself a generous Black Grouse with a splash of water and took it to my bed where I sat back on a pile of pillows. First, I tried to imagine what it might have been like in the tunnels during a nuclear war. Would communications across the country have survived the hellish fall-out? Or would they have been trapped underground and isolated, unable to establish what was happening without exposing themselves to the risk of contamination. Presumably they had tanks of fresh water and generators to keep the lights and other electrical equipment going. But would they have had to abandon their families and loved ones in order to do their duty? And could they really have marshalled the forces of law-and-order to prevent looting and anarchy from their underground lair? How would they have organised medical aid and food for the millions of people in the huge conurbations nearby - people who were now being killed by radiation even if they had survived the initial blast. It didn't bear thinking about. I sipped my whisky for comfort. It was smooth and aromatic, surprisingly lovely for a blended Scotch. Definitely worthy of joining the single malts as a weekend tipple, and a high-end dram for weekdays too.

Then I turned back time and tried to picture the tunnel complex as a hive of manufacturing activity with lorries coming and going all the time, delivering raw materials and taking away completed parts for assembly into engines elsewhere. The lorries would actually drive in and out of the four main tunnels for loading and unloading. The noise must have been incredible and amplified in the tunnels as lathes turned and metal on metal screeched and squealed. What a feat of organisation it must have been. And how could you stay sane, working, relaxing and sleeping underground for such long periods of time? These people would normally be living in the terraced housing of Greater Birmingham, working in brightly lit factories to manufacture up-market cars, and going home for their tea each day or to the pubs on street corners. It made me realise how a country caught up in a seemingly endless World War was forced to reorganise almost every single aspect of how it operated in order to survive and prevail. I reflected that the few petty sacrifices demanded of people to defeat the recent Covid pandemic seemed completely trivial by comparison. I had another swallow of my smoky, spicy drink.

And what must it have been like to build the place? I tried to picture the dust and dirt-filled tunnels with men using explosives to work their way onwards, through the danger-filled darkness. Did they sense the weight of the earth pressing down above them? And then there was the gruelling hard labour of removing the stones and debris. And yet they had hollowed out a complex grid of galleries and chambers, tunnels, and underground rooms sufficient to house a modern engineering factory. Moreover, the grid design meant it would be strong enough to withstand a direct hit by a German bomb. It was an amazing feat of engineering. And it took just eighteen months to complete. I thought back to the people who had lost their lives at that time - five labourers, a security officer, and a woman who 'died of shock'. What of those two men who had died while they were riding the conveyor belt? How old were they? There was no reference to their ages or their names in the information I had read. Someone must know. Were they now just a sad footnote on someone's ancestry website and a neglected grave and headstone in the corner of a local churchyard? Had they been doing it for a lark or a bet? Or was there some other reason to be doing such a dangerous thing? It must have been a horrible way to die.

And what now? Did The Millionaire Tunnels become some kind of museum in the end? And why was there no reference to a warehouse? Was it even there? Perhaps Nick's workplace was elsewhere, somewhere with even more secrecy and less of a fascinating past. It was a puzzle. I checked my watch. Quarter to six. Perhaps I could find out more on Magic Meg in fifteen minutes.

I drained the last of my Scotch and debated whether to take Eddie or not. He'd be quite happy guarding the boat on his own. But I wondered if he might also be a useful icebreaker. Nick had seemed mildly amused by him in the pub, and I wanted the young man to relax enough to give me more information this evening. Yes, I would take a bottle of wine and my little dog to the tarot reading. Eddie would have another glimpse into the follies and failings of the human species.

CHAPTER 5

Nick opened the door at the stern of Magic Meg and backed down the stairs so that Eddie and I could follow him inside. There were hardly any lights on, but I could see that the boat's layout was almost the opposite of Jumping Jack Flash. The galley was positioned immediately after the stairs with a built-in dining table beyond that. I could just about make out a big cluster of floor cushions in the saloon area before a door that must lead towards the bow and the bathroom and sleeping quarters. Everything looked a bit grubby and well-worn and there was a pervading smell of damp which a smouldering joss stick couldn't disguise. I guessed that it had been quite a while since Magic Meg had been taken out of the water and given a good overhaul. A small fire was struggling to catch light in a corner stove, and it was cold enough for my breath to steam.

Nick gave me a sardonic smile, bowed low to me like an Elizabethan courtier and rolled his hand over extravagantly. "Sir, Madame Heloise awaits the company of any seeker after the hidden truth." Then he put a flat hand next to one side of his mouth, winked at me and stage-whispered, "… and fifty quid in cash." I think it was that moment when I finally decided that I didn't like him very much. His girlfriend had seemed perfectly open, genuine and friendly in the pub while he now came across as sarcastic, disbelieving and amused that anyone might part with money for such nonsense. Heloise could do better, I thought, whilst also admitting to a level of cynicism about the whole process myself. But then, I wasn't her boyfriend.

I pressed a bottle of red into his hand. "Here's a tip in advance."

"Great. Thanks very much. Step this way, sir."

Heloise was sitting on a bench seat covered in worn vinyl on the far side of the rectangular table. I shuffled along a similar seat opposite her, with my back to the stern. Eddie curled up at my feet. The table had been covered with a green felt cloth and there was a single pack of yellow-backed cards on it. She smiled at me, and I found it hard not to stare at the piercing blue of her eyes. "Hello Jack, thank you for coming. It's a shame Nina couldn't be here too."

"She went off early this morning to see her mum, but she sends her regards."

Nick put three glass beakers onto the edge of the table. They were badly smeared, but he twisted the metal cap off my wine and sloshed out three generous measures. "Cheers," he said, and we all clinked them together and took a swallow.

"Right then, off you go Nick," said Heloise, pointing to the bow. "I don't want you sniggering in the background."

"Alright," he said grudgingly, "but don't forget, I'm off as soon as it's over. He gave me a look which suggested that I would be expected to leave at the same time.

"Oh yes," I said, as though suddenly remembering, "I was going to ask you both something first. I've been reading up on local history. I always do that when I moor up at a new place. I was fascinated to come across something about The Millionaire Tunnels near here – under a nature reserve called the Millions. They were built as a shadow Rover factory making aircraft parts and then they were equipped as a nuclear bunker. They sound really interesting. I wondered if you knew any more about them?"

Heloise rolled her eyes. "Oh God, now you'll set him off. Nick's an expert on the tunnels. He spends all his working life down there and then he goes back as a volunteer to show people around the museum bit."

"Really?" I said, looking disingenuously at Nick. "Your working life?"

"Most of them are rented out as a warehouse now," he said

matter-of-factly. "I'm on the security team there, but we're not supposed to talk about it. If you want to find out more about their history, you should come on one of the public tours. We show people around the part that we're turning into a museum. You can book a place on Facebook. They last about an hour. There's one the day after tomorrow actually. It's in the morning. I can't do it though. I'll be working so it'll be the B team." He seemed to take my interest at face value and was more than happy to act as a condescending expert on the subject in front of his girlfriend.

"That's a good idea," said Heloise. "You could take Nina if she's back. I've been and it was really interesting – although there isn't much historical stuff down there any more. Now then, let's get started." She wafted a hand at Nick. "Shoo. There's no room for disbelievers at this table." Too late for that, I thought to myself, as Nick wandered off through a swing door towards the bow. I noticed that he took his glass and my bottle of red wine with him.

Heloise picked up the pack of cards and expertly shuffled them for a minute or so. Then she put the deck down on the table and split it into three separate stacks. "First of all, there's nothing to be worried about. Everyone is psychic up to a point. It's just that I've trained myself to have a more developed kind of sixth sense. It's just like a musician or an artist training themselves to be better at playing music or painting. The cards help me to create a bridge between our conscious and unconscious minds. That's all. But we have to respect them and be sympathetic to them."

I nodded warily. "Do you mind if I take notes?" I asked. "Nina wants a full report."

"That's fine."

I pulled a little red notebook and biro out of my jacket pocket and put them beside me on the table.

"Choose one of these piles please, Jack." I pointed to the middle one. She picked it up and inspected the bottom card, wrinkled her nose and replaced my pile of cards on top of the other two. Then she shuffled them thoroughly again before peeling 12 cards from the top which she placed face up in front of her. The cards were carefully arranged in three horizontal rows and four vertical columns. She named each card as she placed it down. The first went top left.

"Mmm, let's see. The Empress – you see she is upside down, so we call that reversed. It's important because it really affects the meaning. Then the Ten of Cups, also reversed. The Queen of Cups, reversed and finally The Lovers ...that's interesting." The last card was the right way up and depicted a nude couple standing in front of two trees. It completed the top row of four cards.

"Now then, the second row. The Nine of Wands, The Four of Pentacles, The Chariot and the Page of Cups, and that's the only reversed card out of those four. And now the last four." She placed a card in the first column under the other two. This showed an old man in a cloak holding a lantern and a staff. Inside the lantern was a six-pointed star. "That's The Hermit and he's reversed," she continued. "Now, who's next? Ah! The Hierophant." I'd never come across this word before, but the picture showed a figure sitting on a throne in a red robe and flanked by two columns. "Now we have the Six of Swords and last but not least, oh, that's strange, Temperance reversed." Temperance looked like an angel standing in a puddle and pouring liquid from one goblet into another. I suspected the liquid would turn out to be water rather than a good single-malt. Heloise looked genuinely puzzled by this final upside-down card at the bottom right-hand corner of the grid.

"Okay then. In for a penny ..." she muttered to herself and drew two more cards which she laid on the table outside the four by three layout. "Hah, The Ace of Cups reversed AND the Seven of Cups reversed. That really is an excess of liquid spirits!" She looked up at me knowingly. "I guess you don't worry too much about counting your alcohol units, Jack," she giggled. I made a mental note to skip over this bit when I described the experience to Nina.

Then she leaned forward over the table and laid both arms flat on top of the left and right-hand columns of cards. She closed her eyes, dipped her head forward and remained quiet for about a minute before snapping her head back and smiling at me. "Right then Jack, let's begin if you're ready?"

"As I'll ever be," I said. I didn't take Eddie's little whimper from below the table as a sign of encouragement.

"We're not just looking at the meaning of particular cards but also their position in relation to the others. The reversed Empress tells me there is an absence of children in your life and I sense this is a sorrow for you, but not one you lose sleep over anymore. I don't see children featuring much in your future either. I'm sorry if that is sad news for you." It was true. The long years of IVF treatment for my ex-wife Debbie and the successive disappointments had left their mental scars - but it was no longer an all-consuming obsession in my life. Good job by the sound of it. I shrugged under the gaze of Hel's sympathetic eyes.

She put the tip of a finger on the reversed Ten of Cups. "You can see this couple with their arms round each other waving at a rainbow with ten cups on it." I could also see two children dancing nearby. "This tells me you've been in an unhappy relationship and I sense that you're divorced. You've also had more recent difficulties in your latest relationship." She looked up at me. "With Nina." It was a statement rather than a question. "But like all reversed cards, it can indicate these problems are being overcome now." That made me sit up. Oxford had been a low point in my friendship with Nina as she grew close to the doomed young American. But I felt as though we had got through it and things had been much more hopeful in recent months. I was still optimistic that we could move on, and that Nina would eventually return my feelings for her.

"And here, see? There's the Four of Pentacles below it which tells me you're in a much better financial position than for quite a while." I nodded at her. The hundred thousand pounds deposited in my bank account for not publishing the account of Zach Hopper's murder and suicide had been the easiest money I had ever earned. I still felt guilty about it – sort of.

"Ah yes. The reversed Queen of Cups followed by The Lovers also tells me there's been a disagreement with your loved one, but you're reconciled now. That's good, isn't it?"

It was true. Nina and I had drifted far apart at Oxford, and I too had found temporary companionship elsewhere. Unfortunately, Nina had guessed as much.

"Now then, the middle row." Her brow creased in concentration as she studied a card that depicted a young man clutching a big wooden staff with eight more planted in the ground behind him. "The Nine of Wands above the reversed Hermit. Look, the young man has a bandaged head. You're going to face a new challenge soon and I feel it will be dangerous – possibly in a cold dark place where you are cut off from others. You must be ready to defend your position, Jack, like the young man with the wands."

I shook my head in bafflement. "Er, okay. Suitably warned."

"And this, The Chariot and the Six of Swords underneath." She closed her eyes. "I'm not sure. But I think there is a journey in your future, a journey featuring a lot of water. Yes, you'll cross a lot of water. It's some kind of sea. But even after you arrive, there will still be water. Be strong and brave and take that journey, Jack. It will truly help you move on in your life. But I am also sensing some kind of confined and narrow space. There's some kind of ordeal you must go through, but it will be worthwhile." I puzzled over this one. Nina and I had been thinking of taking a trip to Amsterdam and staying on a houseboat for a couple of weeks. But there's no way Heloise could have known this. I saw the door behind her open and close quietly as Nick sidled into the room and stood by it. He put a finger to his mouth. He didn't want me to reveal his presence to his girlfriend.

"Lastly, The Hierophant," she said. This was the card with a figure sitting in a robe on a throne. "Some people also call this one the High Priest or the Pope. You're going to have an encounter with the spiritual world quite soon, Jack. Somehow, you're going to connect with the unseen and the unworldly. Or they are going to connect with you. But don't worry, they're going to be benign. You can trust them."

"I'm going to meet a ghost?" I asked disbelievingly.

"That's what the cards are telling me." She smiled and winked. "But then they also told me you're no stranger to spirits of a different kind!"

"Ha ha, very funny. Well, that was um, interesting. Of course, I can't know if your predictions will come true, but some of the rest of it rang true. Um…thank you."

She was already gathering her cards together and wrapping them gently in a black silk cloth. "You're welcome, Jack. Perhaps Nina would like me to read her cards when she gets back?'

"Oh, I'm absolutely certain she will," I said mischievously and drained the remnants of my wine before taking out my wallet and putting five ten-pound notes on the table. "There you go. Fifty pounds as agreed." Not bad for 15 minutes work, I thought to myself privately. Heloise picked up the money just as Nick arrived beside us. I was still a sceptic, perhaps even a cynic, but I had also been surprised by some of the accuracy of her comments. She clearly needed the money for Magic Meg and I didn't begrudge paying her.

"All finished then. Go well, did it?" Nick didn't wait for an answer. I noticed that he hadn't returned with the bottle of red. He rubbed his hands together. "Right then, time to go. I'll see you later Hel. Places to go, things to do, people to see." There clearly wasn't going to be any small talk. He bent down to kiss her on the lips. "After you, Jack."

"Thanks again Jack," said Heloise.

"No, thank you Hel. It's been quite an experience. Lots to think about." I strolled slowly back to my boat, fed Eddie and fried myself a steak. I poured a pan of hot baked beans over it. I'm a lazy cook when Nina isn't around. Then I poured myself a generous measure of the Black Grouse and slumped into an armchair just as my phone pinged to indicate an incoming text. It was Nina.

"*Hi. How did the reading go?*"

"*She's nice,*" I typed back. "*But Nick's a dick.*" I added an emoji – a face with upward rolling eyes.

My phone pinged again. *"What did she say?"*

"Be easier to tell you. Are you free to talk?"

My phone rang a minute later, and a photo of Nina filled the screen with her big beautiful dark eyes and short black hair. "I'll have to be quick. I've got some food on the hob for mummy."

"How is she?"

"Struggling to get about. But there's a new carer starting tomorrow so I'll stay to make sure mummy isn't beastly to her and come back the day after."

That was sooner than I'd dared to hope. "Great!"

"So come on then, tell me about the tarot cards."

I took a deep breath. "Well, some of it was very accurate. She said I'd come into some money recently, that I … well, that Deb and me had struggled to have children. She said you and I had had … um … difficulties recently but that we were getting over that." I paused, hoping for a response but there was silence. "You still there?"

"Yes, Jack. Go on." Her tone was completely neutral.

"Oh, okay. She said we'd go abroad soon, over water to somewhere with lots of water – so that could be Amsterdam, couldn't it?"

"That's weird. We were talking about it only last week, weren't we?"

"Yes. There's no way she could have known about that. Anyway, she also said I'd face some kind of challenge in a cold, dark space."

"Oh. I don't like the sound of that. Anything else?"

"There was some mumbo jumbo about some kind of spectral encounter."

"Weird. Anything else?"

"She said I drank too much," I muttered.

"What?" she laughed. "Really?"

"Yes, there were all these bloody cup cards and a reversed one called Temperance."

Nina was still laughing. "Oh, that's too much! Even the cards agree with me!"

"I reckon you paid her extra to say that."

"No, she's obviously just very perceptive."

"Well, that's alright then, because I've booked you in for a reading when you get back."

"You haven't!"

"I have," I lied. "So, we can lift the lid on all your little secrets, can't we?"

"Except I haven't got any Jack. Look, I'm sorry, but I'm going to have to go."

"Oh – there was one other thing. It turns out Nick the Dick is a security guard in some tunnels near here and they have been turned into a warehouse. So that must be where the silver is being stored. But part of it is also a museum and you can do tours. There's one the day after tomorrow so I might get some tickets and have a look. They've got a fascinating history. Six people died when they were being built, then they were used as an underground factory in the war, and then …"

"It all sounds fascinating, Jack. I love it when you get obsessed by something – but I've got to go. I'll see you the day after tomorrow hopefully. I'll let you know when I'm getting in – although I've got my spare key."

"Oh. Okay. Sure. See you Thursday."

"Bye Jack," she trilled, and the line went dead.

Eddie looked up at me mournfully. I ruffled his ears. "Don't fret old chap. She'll be back soon. I had one more Scotch before bed. But before I turned the light out, I opened up Facebook and spent £6.50 on a ticket for the tour of The Millionaire Tunnels Museum at 12 noon on Thursday. If Nina turned up on Thursday morning, I could always try to buy another one.

CHAPTER 6

I slept badly that night, in spite of my relatively sober evening. A sporadic drumbeat of acorns cracked down onto the boat's roof from the overhanging branches of a mature oak. I tossed and turned in my bed while the words of Heloise went round and round in my head. I had my scribbled notes, but now I wished I had recorded the reading too. What exactly did she say about me and Nina? There was something about a reversed card indicating our difficulties were behind us. But that was a bit vague, wasn't it? And it wasn't exactly promising sunlit uplands, was it? I lay there and brooded until about 2 a.m. when it began to rain very heavily. I cursed myself for not asking more questions.

The noise of the acorns was now drowned out by the continuous rumble of rainwater hitting the roof. I have always found the sound of rain falling at night to be comforting and I'm not alone. I had seen a biopic of the American comedian, W.C. Fields, and I was surprised to discover that he also felt like me. He was dying in a sanatorium on Christmas Day, 1946, when a woman friend comforted him by using a garden hose to simulate rain on the roof of his room. The change to my nocturnal soundtrack, from the acorns to the rain, finally sent me off into a fitful slumber.

A glance out of the porthole told me it had stopped raining by the time I woke up. I shivered into my dressing gown, padded to the loo and then to the galley to boil a kettle. There is a window on both sides of the galley and I could see across the canal to the curious rectangular space that had been cut in the cliff-face opposite Jumping Jack Flash. The water all around my mooring had been covered by a carpet of brown, green and yellow leaves on the previous day. But I couldn't see any of them now because the canal was covered by a layer of mist that clung to its surface. It was almost like being in the window seat of an aeroplane, staring down at an unbroken sea of cloud below. There was something slightly magical about it – as though a lady's hand holding a sword might suddenly rise out of the vapour at any moment. I shook my head and sipped my coffee. Snap out of it, Jack. Stop daydreaming and get yourself moving.

I had decided to take Eddie up onto Kinver Edge for a good walk that morning. My Ordnance Survey map showed an enticing expanse of green stretching away to the south of the town and the red initials of the National Trust next to somewhere called Holy Austin Rock. The sky had brightened, and my weather app said it was going to be a largely dry day. I switched to googling the Trust's website for Kinver Edge and studied it as I munched on a bowl of blueberries and muesli. Nina was waging a continuous war against my regular breakfast of bacon rolls, and she seemed to be winning.

The Edge was two miles long and 500 feet high, surrounded by 579 acres of wood and lowland heath. The land, according to the website, was made up of Bunter pebble beds, (whatever they were), and the red sandstone I had already seen in the little cliffs alongside the canal. This stone had been created 200 million years ago out of wind-blown sand dunes and its soft but stable nature made it easy to excavate. Hence The Millionaire Tunnels, I thought to myself. The website also explained that Holy Austin Rock was some kind of collection of cave homes that had been carved out of the sandstone and were open to the public. It all sounded fascinating and so I put a couple of poo bags in my pocket along with some gravy bones and set off, with Eddie running on ahead along the towpath.

We left the canal at The Vine, traversed the High Street, and climbed a long straight road that rose out of town. A row of cars was parked at right angles to the road next to a cluster of signs pointing into the countryside which advertised the National

Trust, Holy Austin Rock and an iron-age hill fort. I had decided to visit the cave homes first, but a friendly young volunteer at the entrance told me dogs weren't allowed inside. "You can grab a coffee if you want and sit outside. And I'll keep an eye on him if you tie him to the table when you go in."

That sounded fine, so I handed over my entrance fee and made my way to a metal table and chair on a small stone terrace. To my left were the facades of three brick-faced and gable-fronted houses that had been built against the cliff face. One of the three front doors was open and I could glimpse a little refreshment counter just inside. I was soon settled outside with a coffee and a bowl of water for Eddie when a smiling middle-aged lady sat down opposite me. A lapel badge told me she was Bessie and a National Trust volunteer guide.

"Hello," she said cheerily. "Have you been here before?" After confessing that I hadn't, she immediately launched into a chatty introduction to the site. "Well, there were 11 families living here by 1861. That's when the Kinver Iron Works down by the canal were at their peak. I think some of the workers, probably the foremen, moved up here to get away from all the noise and dirt." She pointed out across the town. "A lot of visitors say how peaceful and green it all looks now, but it must have been a mucky old place then. The Foley family used the river, the Stour, to power their iron mills - which they used to make nails. And their nails made them a fortune. And the canal was built in 1772 by James Brindley to serve the ironworks."

"Yes, I've got a boat. I'm moored on the canal for the moment."

"Oh really? It's lovely down there now, isn't it? Well, the village prospered but the ironworks only lasted 50 years. Luckily for us, the tourists and day trippers started coming a bit later and they've been coming ever since. A light-railway, like a tram, was installed down by the river in 1901 and 4 years later there were 17,000 visitors in just one day." She shook her head. "It was amazing really."

"They came to see the cave homes?" I asked.

"Oh yes, and to have tea and cakes and walk on the Edge. Just like now. But there were people living in these homes even then. It must have felt like living in a zoo! There are the upper houses, a middle level and a lower level. You can go inside at the top and the bottom. Look out for the well outside the bottom cottages. It was the deepest private well in Britain once – 180 ft deep. We'll keep an eye on this little lad, while you're gone, won't we boy?" Eddie put both his forepaws on her thigh in appreciation and was rewarded with a pat on his otter-like head.

"Thanks. Thanks very much. I won't be long." I decided to start at the bottom and found two cosy little cottages that had been carved out of the rock and faced with brick. A small fire blazed in a cast-iron cooking range and a painting of an elderly couple sitting by the window showed that the interior had been faithfully recreated. Between the cottages, a large, long rectangular space called The Ballroom had been excavated. A Trust sign told me that the walls and ceilings were washed with lime once a year to control dust, make them brighter and act as a disinfectant. It was almost incredible to think people were still living in these caves half-way through the last century. I took a few pictures on my phone to send to Nina.

Bessie was still sitting at my table and making a fuss of Eddie when I returned. "They're astonishing," I said to her. "Why did people leave them in the end?"

"Oh, they were falling down by the time the Trust took them over," she said. "And, well … let's just say the toilet arrangements were a bit basic. But the restoration has been very accurate. The Trust saved the homes, and the locals keep them going."

"If you're a local, you must know all about The Millionaire Tunnels," I said.

"Oh yes. In fact, my father worked in them during the war. But he didn't talk about it much. That generation didn't really, did they?"

"Well, I've bought a ticket for the tour."

"Oh, yes. There's not much left down there now, but they're worth seeing."

"Well, I must be going – Eddie and I need to be off on our

walk." Bessie told me to wait a second while she fetched a more detailed map of Kinver Edge. About two-thirds of it appeared to be wooded and one-third heathland. She showed me a path from the hill fort to another cave home called Nanny's Rock, and then advised me to explore the heath.

"Just make sure little Eddie doesn't find an adder," she warned.

Thankfully, there was no encounter with a snake as Eddie and I enjoyed a couple of hours exploring this unique part of the county border between Staffordshire and Worcestershire. The sunshine was weak but nonetheless welcome.

We were roughly halfway along our route and standing outside a natural cavern called Nanny's Rock when a strange thing happened. A family emerged from inside one of the caves, chattering excitedly together in a foreign language. It was a couple with a young girl, perhaps four or five years old. They were each holding her by a hand and swinging her forwards and backwards with her feet off the ground. It was a charming, cheerful sight. As they came near me, I realised that I recognised the man. It was the waiter from my lunch yesterday. The one who hurried away in a panic when I asked him about the tunnels. He was only five metres away when he looked up and clearly recognised me too.

"It's you again. What do you want?" he demanded immediately as he moved to stand protectively in front of his wife. She peered at me worriedly from behind him. The child was looking up at them both in puzzlement at the abrupt ending of her game. "Why do you follow me?" he demanded angrily.

I tried to calm him down by holding both my palms towards him with my fingers spread wide. "I'm sorry. I don't know why I upset you yesterday. Please, don't worry about it."

But the man was already ushering his little family away with his arm around his wife, and his little girl was being dragged along by the hand. He shot anxious glances back at me over his shoulder as they moved away, back along the path towards the hill fort. Once again, he looked frightened and suspicious.

I puzzled over this brief incident as we began to walk back to the boat. The man clearly perceived me as some kind of threat. A threat to him and his family. But why? I had never seen him before in my life. It was very odd. I contemplated turning around and trying to catch him up. I could demand an explanation. I should have done so at the time. But no, the sight of me hurrying in his wake might make the situation even worse. I shrugged. There was nothing to be done. But I do hate an unexplained mystery and the encounter snagged at my brain all the way back to the boat.

CHAPTER 7

I dozed and read a crime novel for the rest of the day before walking along to The Vine with Eddie. I didn't feel like cooking so planned on having a couple of pints and an evening meal there. It was a sprawling pub with a large garden, and it was obviously well set up to cater for the large crowds of summer visitors to the town. A text arrived from Nina while I was waiting for my chicken korma.

"*Need to stay one more day,*" it read. "*See you Friday xx.*"

I texted back a thumbs-up emoji and a single kiss. No point in overdoing it. She needed to know I was feeling a bit fed up with her newly extended absence. This also meant I would be doing the tunnel tour on my own. Ah well, I could tell her all about it and show her some pictures on my phone.

Except I couldn't. Having followed the Facebook directions to the tunnel's entrance on the following day, I joined a group of people milling around outside and was handed a piece of paper which said all photography was forbidden. This was curious. There were pictures on The Millionaire Tunnels website that showed parts of the underground complex. So why couldn't I take any? A middle-aged man in a yellow tabard was standing by a thick, metal door in the entrance to the tunnel. I made to approach him and ask for an explanation, but there was a sudden yank on Eddie's lead. The little dog had put on the handbrake and was refusing to budge a step closer to the tunnels. I gave him a sharp tug, but Eddie stood firm and then started whining loudly. He was staring at the open door, but he obviously had no desire to go any closer. A few people near me turned to enjoy the scene he was making. When terriers make up their mind like this, they're hard to budge. A bit like Nina, I thought to myself.

I bent down to comfort him. "What's up, old boy. You don't mind going underground, do you?" This was ironic, I thought to myself. Border terriers were originally bred to be sent down fox tunnels when the hunt's quarry went to earth. But Eddie looked genuinely scared at the prospect and continued to protest.

The tour guide in the tabard came over to me. "It's a good job he doesn't want to come in, because he's not allowed anyway." He pointed to the paper in my hand. "It's all there in black and white. No dogs I'm afraid." I glanced down the list of dos and don'ts for Millionaire Tunnel Visitors and cursed myself for not checking the small print before I came. Luckily, a couple were standing nearby and they had overhead our conversation. The woman bent down and patted Eddie.

"Ah, that's a shame isn't it," she said, in a strong Birmingham accent. "You walked here, didn't you? We've got a car parked just over there. You can put him in the back if you like. He'll be fine for an hour, won't he?"

I accepted the offer gratefully. Eddie eagerly retreated from the tunnel's entrance and jumped into the roomy boot of their SUV. The guide was joined by another younger man who marshalled us into a tighter group by the door. He counted heads. "Ten in all. That's right," he announced, looking down at his paperwork.

"Right then, let's get going," said the older man. He told us to stay together and not to wander off from the main group and he warned about the danger of trip hazards in the tunnel doorways. I noticed a couple of people in the group were carrying torches. Surely that wouldn't be necessary?

We were entering the complex through the entrance to Adit B, he said. This wasn't one of the four main tunnel entrances, but it gave direct access to the museum part of the complex. Immediately beyond the heavy metal door were some side rooms with rubber suits hanging up. It appeared to be some kind of decontamination chamber. We trailed into the tunnel on the other side of the entrance passageway. It was slightly arched towards the top. I put my hand on the wall and was surprised that it didn't feel damp to the touch. It was cool and dry and pitted with long indentations. "Those are the marks left by the pneumatic drills," said the guide. "They took 35 million cubic feet of sandstone out of here on conveyor belts." These were the same conveyor belts that had killed two men, I thought to myself.

We walked past World War II posters – one had a pilot on it asking, 'Can You Help Me? Build A Plane". Then we entered a sick bay with rusting metal beds and old medicine cabinets. The guide paused to tell the group about the six people who had been killed during the construction phase of the tunnel and about the constant risk of injury from the factory's machinery.

We moved on into a large canteen area. The stainless steel of the serving counter looked surprisingly new. "It's never been used," said the guide. "They put it in for the politicians and civil servants in the event of a nuclear war. There would have been about 300 of them down here. Alright for some, eh?" I had drifted to the rear of the group and looked up at the stone ceiling of the large square room. Strangely, two gothic-looking black iron candelabra hung down from it.

"They look a bit out of place," I said to the young guide who was shepherding the tour from behind.

He looked up and shrugged. "They're left over from the paranormal groups. They used to come down here and do seances and stuff. Lot more atmospheric by candlelight I suppose. But they're not allowed now. Strictly banned."

"Oh? Why's that?" I asked.

"The warehouse, I suppose." He nodded ahead to where a new and recent looking wall of breeze blocks sealed off the tunnel we were in. "Ninety per cent of the tunnels are rented to a warehouse firm now. They probably don't want people running around down here on their own. Although you can't get in there from this bit, obviously."

I was keen to learn more, but the group was being urged to stay together and keep moving. Lights were suspended from rusty girders which spanned some of the rooms we were in. I had been right. There was no need for torches – unless there was a power-cut. But surely, there would be emergency generators, I thought. I certainly wouldn't fancy being trapped down here in pitch blackness.

We walked on, past dormitories lined with metal-framed beds, offices with rusting desks, chairs and filing cabinets and even a little room earmarked as a small BBC studio. An old bit of transmission equipment with a microphone sat on a desk below a window looking into a producer's booth. It had a fading BBC Radio Shropshire logo on it. We were told it would have broadcast to five and a half million people across the Midlands if nuclear weapons had been dropped. Although, I supposed its usefulness would have depended on whether the blast had also destroyed the above-ground transmitter masts.

In another area, the remains of a 1940s tannoy system had been pushed up against one wall. "They used it to play music and make announcements to the factory's workforce," said the guide. "Of course, it's not working now."

At one point, the guide stopped and told us to look up at the ceiling. I couldn't see anything unusual. "Look at the pipes," he said. "Of course, with so many tunnels and so many people down here, you have to circulate fresh air. There have been three different systems over the years. The first smaller pipe was for the aircraft parts factory. You can see it on the left up there. Then that was replaced and upgraded to the bigger round pipe next to it. That was for the nuclear bunker. And now you can see the latest system." A big square aluminium duct sat impressively alongside the smaller round pipes. "That's been put in by the warehouse people next door. Any questions? Right. Let's move on this way, shall we?"

The group began to shuffle forwards again, with me at the rear alongside the second younger guide. There were three men in front of me, all wearing baseball caps. I had noticed them earlier and been quietly amused by their very different physiques. One was tall and thin, another was quite big and fat and the third was quite short. I had mentally dubbed them Boggis, Bunce and

Bean after the farmers in one of my favourite books, Fantastic Mr Fox by Roald Dahl. I guessed that they were all aged in their early thirties and all three were dressed identically in dark jeans and fleeces. The other six people on the tour were all couples, including the friendly pair who had provided their car for Eddie. The man in the middle of the trio, the tallest, suddenly pulled a mobile phone out of his pocket and held it up in in front of him.

"Quick selfie," he said. "Smile for the camera boys." There was something strange about his accent. South African perhaps? The other two crowded their heads in close to his and looked down at the upward pointing phone. The camera's fake shutter sound repeated itself as he fired off a rapid succession of snaps.

"Hey, no pictures!" called out the tour guide from behind me.

The man with the phone turned to look back over his shoulder. "Oh yeah. Sorry man. I forgot. Me bad." He shook his head as though confessing to his stupidity and immediately pocketed the phone.

We continued the tour, pausing to look at a large black-and-white aerial picture of some Swiss looking buildings. These, we learnt, had all been demolished so that there was no overhead clue to the tunnels' locations. We peered through a few more doorways to inspect large square water tanks and other bits of infrastructure before making our way back outside. I saw the three couples putting a few coins in a slotted box near the door which was labelled 'Tunnel Preservation Fund'. I posted a fiver into it, but the group of three men ignored it and hurried away towards the car park. I looked at my watch. Five past one. Lunchtime. They were probably in a rush to get to a pub. We had been underground for nearly an hour.

"Thanks very much. That was really interesting," I said to the two guides who were lighting up cigarettes outside.

"Thanks for coming," said the younger one. "We've got lots to do to the display areas, but it's an important part of our history round here and it needs saving."

"Aye," nodded the older man. "And we're recording interviews with anyone who worked here or has a connection."

I told them about Bessie, the volunteer at Holy Austin Rock and her father who'd worked in the factory. Then I glanced over to see the couple waiting patiently for me by their car. "So, what kind of stuff does the warehouse store?" I asked as innocently as possible.

"Search me," said the younger volunteer. "It's all very hush hush. CCTV and guards everywhere."

"I think the lady in the sari wants you to fetch your dog," said the older man.

CHAPTER 8

Boat traffic gets pretty quiet on the canals as temperatures drop, but I still noticed a few craft going past my mooring - perhaps one or two every hour. Now that I was an experienced skipper and liveaboard, I was regularly frustrated by the antics of less considerate boaters. I would fume when I found a boat moored up on a lock landing. This is a section of the towpath above or below a lock which needs to be kept free so boats can wait to enter the lock or let crew off to operate it.

But the top of my hate list are boats that refuse to slow down as they go past your mooring. It's simple good manners to reduce engine speed to a tick over and go past without creating much of a wash. However, some boats – and they aren't all holiday hires – shoot past and their bow wave sends your boat rocking violently. I've even had my mooring pegs pulled out of the ground by one idiot who clearly thought he was in a James Bond movie. The most common culprits seem to be men of a certain age who ought to know better.

My longest-serving friend, a professional actor called Will, had stayed on the boat for a week during the recent summer. He had brought the latest in an ever-changing procession of girlfriends for a week's holiday and luckily, the young actress got on well with Nina. However, Will too became enraged at the lack of etiquette displayed by some passing boats – especially when one vigorous rocking made him spill a full glass of gin and tonic into his lap. He leapt to his feet, ran to the bow and bellowed after the speeding tillerman at the top of his theatre-trained voice. "HEY, YOU STUPID BASTARD. WHAT GOOD IS SPEED IF YOUR BRAIN

HAS OOZED OUT ON THE WAY?" His voice had the clear diction necessary to be heard at the back of the Upper Stalls.

He came back inside and bowed to a round of applause from the three of us. He deftly stooped to the floor,
scooped up the lemon slice from his spilt drink, straightened and grinned at us. "Karl Kraus, an Austrian satirist, don't y'know?" We discovered that he'd been looking through my Oxford Dictionary of Quotations and had compiled a list of relevant abuse. And so, for the rest of the week, Will treated any speeding boater to a similar earbashing from his collection.

I think my favourite took place one warm July evening when we were all sitting and chatting in the well deck. I could tell from the sound of an approaching engine that it was going to be a bumpy one. Will jumped up onto the bow with his feet straddling the boat, spread his arms wide and roared at the passing helmswoman: "AND COME HE SLOW, AND COME HE FAST, IT IS BUT DEATH WHO COMES AT LAST. SO SLOW DOWN YOU STUPID BINT!" She looked startled at him, mouthed "Sorry", and immediately reduced her revs.

On the evening before their last day, Will made a little performance of presenting me with his scribbled quotations. I laughed and shook my head. "No, I don't think so Will. I don't think I've got the chutzpah or the voice to carry it off."

"Ah," he said with a sly look. "I thought you might say that, my old love. So, I've got something else for you instead." He leant down, reached into his shoulder bag and pulled out a long thin package taped up in wrapping paper. "Go on, open it. It's a present to say thank you for having us. And it isn't a bottle of whisky," he added, looking at Nina with a grin.

I unwrapped my surprise present. It looked like a gun of some kind. "You want me to shoot them?" I said incredulously.

His evil smile reminded me of the picture of Jumping Jack Flash on the side of my boat. "Yep. With these." He held up a see-through bag which seemed to be full of small red and blue balls, the size of marbles. "It's a paint-ball gun. I got it from a second-hand shop in town. So, when you're moored up and some dingbat speeds past, just reach for this and plop a red mark on their back. It'll be their mark of everlasting shame. And it'll make you feel better. It doesn't actually last for ever, of course. Just till the next wash cycle."

It sounded daft to me and a sure-fire way of getting myself into a fight. And, of course, 'head-girl' Nina was horrified by the idea of meting out summary retribution in this way. But the following morning, we all watched as Will raced manically through the length of the boat to emerge at the bow as a passing boat continued to speed past us. Our boat was rocking furiously. He waited until there was about twenty feet of clear water between us and the target and then fired. A red smudge appeared smack between the shoulder blades of the retreating skipper's back. The man looked left and right and then behind him, but Will had already ducked back inside. Will's girlfriend was amused, and Nina was aghast, but I was excited.

He insisted that I should have a go if another speedster went by before he left. In the event, the rocking boat put me off my aim and I left it too late to fire. We all watched the paint ball shoot harmlessly over the target's head and into the water beyond. But I confess, there have been times since when my annoyance has reached boiling point and I have reached for the gun. Needless to say, this only happens when Nina isn't on board.

After four days on my current mooring, I was starting to get very fed up with the number of passing boats that were going too fast. I had scribbled PLEASE SLOW DOWN on two pieces of cardboard which I had propped up at the stern and the bow – but there was little sign of them working. The final straw came on Thursday afternoon, when one particularly vigorous shaking set Eddie off barking. The rocking and the barking woke me up from a delicious afternoon nap, and it made me very grumpy.

I stomped to a chair next to the little French doors that lead out to the well deck and sat there, like a spider waiting for a fly. My loaded gun was cradled in my lap. The next few boats were well-mannered, and so I picked up my book to pass the time. About an hour later I heard loud rap-music approaching fast. Boaters who are inconsiderate about noise also tend to be inconsiderate about their speed too. I poked my head above the roof and looked back along the length of Jumping Jack Flash. Two youngish men were standing at the tiller of a boat that was pushing up a moustache-shaped froth of water where its bow met the surface of the canal. They were laughing and joking and paying very little attention to my cardboard sign or their speed. I ducked back inside and closed the doors until there was just a small gap left between them. I pushed the gun barrel through the crack, squinted along its sight and waited.

Sure enough, my boat started bucking almost as soon as the newcomer had come alongside. Eddie barked, which is a sure sign of a speed violation. I waited and squeezed off a ball almost as soon as the backs of both men appeared. Oops. An upward movement of the boat's deck had raised my gun in that split instant. The shot would probably have missed, but I had fired too quickly and so there was insufficient space between us. A red splodge exploded on the back of the nearest man's neck, rather than in the centre of his fleece where I had been aiming. I saw him slap a palm onto his neck and look at the red paint on his hand. He must have thought it was blood. He looked round in shock just before I dropped to the deck like a stone. Damnation. What an idiot. Had I, literally, just been caught red-handed? I kneeled up and risked a peep through the glass of the door.

The two men were talking excitedly and clearly failing to pay attention to their course. Their boat seemed to be going even faster. It collided quite hard with the towpath bank and scraped along before they hit reverse gear and stopped dead in the water. The music and the engine were switched off in the same moment and quiet descended on the mooring. It was an uneasy peace for me. I quickly stowed the paintball gun under my bed and reopened my novel. Eddie was giving me one of his curious head tilts, and then moments later he barked as a voice called out. "Hello. Hello, is anyone there?"

I kept hold of my book and went out onto the well deck. The two young men were standing on the bank. They looked worryingly gym fit. "Hi," I said.

"Hi. My mate's just been hit on the neck by a paint ball."

"Yeah, and it bloody stung," said his friend, turning around to show me a fist-sized splodge of red above his fleece. "I thought I was bleeding at first."

"D'you know anything about it?"

I looked up and around our mooring as nonchalantly as possible and pointed vaguely to the trees on the opposite bank and the road beyond. "Bloody kids, I expect. "You've been ambushed. Although they haven't troubled me." I was starting to feel guilty now. These two lads seemed pretty harmless and maybe they just hadn't been told about the tick-over-to-overtake rule. I tried a smile to lighten the mood. "Maybe they didn't like your music?"

"So, it wasn't you then?" asked the one who had been shot.

"Me?" I tried to act shocked. "Don't be silly. I was quietly reading my book with Eddie here." I glanced along at their boat and a thought suddenly occurred to me. It wouldn't hurt to change the subject either. "I see you've got a little dinghy on your roof."

"Yeah, it's my dad's boat. We've just borrowed it for a couple of days."

"Would you let me hire the dinghy for an hour? I'll pay cash."

"What for?" asked the red neck.

"How much?" asked his friend.

"There's a little boathouse back there called Devil's Den. It's a little wooden door in a cliff on the far side of the canal. No towpath. I thought I'd like to take a look at it. It won't take long, and I'll give you twenty quid cash. That'll pay for a few drinks in the pub tonight." And compensate you for a stinging neck, I thought to myself.

The two lads looked at each other and then back at me. Red neck shrugged. "It's alright by me. Twenty quid you say?"

"We might as well moor up for the night now anyway," said his friend. "It'll be dark soon."

"Okay, you fetch the dinghy and some paddles, and I'll get the money."

They walked back to their boat, muttering quietly between themselves and casting rueful glances up into the trees opposite. I watched them use a foot pump to put more air into the little rubber boat. Then they carried it back to me and on around the bend where they placed it in the water opposite the little black wooden door. "Would one of you mind paddling?" I asked. "It'll make it easier for me to land and have a look around."

"I'll do it," said red neck. I noticed that he had washed the paint off now, but there was a sore-looking penny-sized mark on his skin which made me feel guilty.

"Great – and would you mind keeping an eye on Eddie?" I said to his friend.

It took a matter of seconds to row across the canal and approach the door to The Devil's Den. I kept us static and steady by holding on to a creeper that draped down one side of the door from the bank above. The right-hand side of the door was flanked by layers of the smooth red sandstone and the intertwining roots of a tree clung to it above. I was surprised to see that no recent graffiti had been carved into it, unlike the outside of the homes at Holy Austin Rock. The stone holding the door had been carefully carved into an arch with hand tools, and water lapped along its bottom edge. If it was an old boathouse, the water would continue down to the bottom of the canal, but it was too dark to tell. The door itself looked solid enough with big metal hinges. Up close, it was bigger than I thought, easily the height of a standing man. A hefty hasp and staple were joined together with a strong-looking padlock.

"My canal guide thinks it was used as a boathouse by the Foley family," I explained to the lad with the paddle. "They were fabulously wealthy ironmasters and they lived near here in a mansion called Prestwood Hall. I tried pushing one door inwards, and then the other, but they refused to budge. I bent backwards to look above the door where there was a slight gap.

"I don't think you'll be climbing up there," my crewmate said.

"No, nor do I." The little cliff rose vertically into a jungle of greenery that would have been impossible to penetrate. I parked any idea of exploring the top or rear of the cave. The entire escapade had taken twenty minutes rather than an hour, but I had scratched an itch and satisfied my curiosity up to a point. I would have loved to have seen inside. How big a space had the workmen hollowed out? Was there any other way into it apart from the waterside door? Were the remains of a gentleman's Victorian rowing skiff rotting somewhere inside? I'd probably never know.

"It's a strange name. The Devil's Den," I said to red neck as he rowed me back to his friend.

"There's a private lake back there," he replied, nodding back in the direction of the aqueduct. I remembered the round pool we had passed on the way to our mooring. "Dad says that's called The Devil's Punchbowl. He reckons the navvies who built the canal were camped there and they had a bad reputation for drinking and poaching and stealing. Maybe it was named after them?"

I thanked the two young men, paid them, shook hands, and watched them wander back to their narrowboat on its mooring up ahead. The paint gun stunt was stupid, I thought to myself as I debated between pouring myself a whisky or a gin. I could have hit the boy in his eye. Yes, I could have blinded him. It didn't bear thinking about. I put the idea of a drink on hold for a moment and recovered the gun. Then I slipped it quietly over the side, into the canal water where it quickly sank out of sight.

"Sorry Will," I said quietly. "Let the magnet fishermen have it". This selfless act made me feel good and so I also decided to postpone my first drink for another hour. Sometimes, my iron self-discipline amazes me.

CHAPTER 9

I spent the following morning running the boat's engine to top up my batteries and Nina arrived just in time for lunch. Eddie greeted her as though she'd been away for a year, jumping excitedly on his hind legs and attempting to lick her face. I followed up, in second place as usual, and gave her a hug and a kiss on one cheek. She updated me on news from home as I heated up some soup and put some bread under the grill for buttered toast.

Then, as we ate, I told her about my sightseeing tours of The Millionaire Tunnels and the Holy Austin Rock houses at Kinver Edge. She seemed genuinely enthusiastic and wanted to see both places for herself. "Well, the houses are open almost all of the time," I said. "But the tunnel tours seem pretty sporadic. I was lucky to catch one."

I showed her the tunnel museum's website and she was intrigued to see the photographs after I told her we weren't allowed to take our own. "But why on earth would they ban you from taking pictures?" she asked, as she surreptitiously palmed a crust of soupy toast into Eddie's mouth.

"I imagine it's to do with the warehouse next door," I said. "Or maybe they think they'll get more visitors if it's all a bit mysterious."

Then Nina urged me to repeat everything from my tarot card reading. I was surprised by her enthusiasm for such nonsense. She has always been so sensible and grounded in the past. Her beautiful eyes always suggested a calm, no-nonsense approach to life. I tried to suggest that Heloise might have picked up information about me on the internet or social media, or from the two books I'd had published about the Midlands Canal Pusher and our time in Bath. But she wasn't having any of it.

"You're just a grumpy old cynic," she said. "I want to get a reading for myself."

"Well, I'm sure she'll be grateful for the money. She needs to spend a bit more on that boat if you ask me."

"You see! Case proven! A cynic is someone who knows the price of everything and the value of nothing."

"Yes, thank you Oscar," I said. "But seriously? Do you really think your future can be told in a random hand of cards?"

She declined to answer this and went off to change out of her smart clothes. Afterwards, we made a plan to wheel our bicycles to the repair shop at Kinver, buy some meat from the High Street butchers and then walk Eddie on the Edge again. But the plan changed after Heloise saw us passing on the towpath and rushed out to meet us. She hopped off the boat and gave Nina a very friendly hug while I struggled to keep Eddie's leash untangled and both bikes upright.

"Hi there," said Nina cheerfully. "Jack told me all about his tarot reading. It all sounded very accurate – especially the bit about his drinking!" They both had a good laugh about that.

"You should have a reading for yourself," said Heloise.

"I want one," said Nina enthusiastically.

"Well, I'm free this afternoon. How about in an hour's time?"

"Great! I'll get some cakes in town." She shot me a mock-guilty look. "You don't mind do you Jack?"

I did mind. I minded a lot. But I also knew it was hopeless trying to dissuade Nina once she had decided on a course of action. I shrugged and handed her back her bike.

"See you in a bit," said Nina, hugging Heloise again. How could women discover new best friends so easily? It baffled me. But then, I don't have many friends beyond Will, Nina and Eddie.

I spent an hour roaming around Kinver Edge on my own after Nina headed back to Magic Meg with a bag of shopping. Eddie darted in and out of the clumps of heather and made friends with a handful of other dogs. He's such an amiable little chap unless he's on his lead and feeling threatened. Then he tries to get his retaliation in first, especially if the other dog is bigger than him.

The curtains were drawn on Magic Meg as I walked past. I thought about knocking but I was pretty certain Nina would be back on Jumping Jack Flash. My own tarot card reading had taken barely quarter of an hour. Nevertheless, there was no sign of her on my boat and I was in a bleak mood by the time she eventually rolled up, an hour and a half later.

"Well, that was a fascinating afternoon," she said laughingly as Eddie leapt around her for the second time that day. "Hel is utterly lovely. We had a good old chinwag, and that cake was excellent. I've saved you a piece."

I grunted. Nina knew I was annoyed with her, but she blithely rattled on.

"She hasn't been with Nick for very long – a couple of months. I think she's got her reservations about him to be honest. He seems to want to control her a bit too much. And he's very jealous. She's only 22. Can you imagine? I thought she looked a little bit older than that. But I'd kill for her eyes. They're such an amazing colour, aren't they? We got on very well. It's a shame we'll be moving on in a way. Perhaps we could stay here a bit longer? Till after Christmas maybe? What d'you think? Jack?"

I had emptied the shopping bag and begun peeling and crushing some garlic cloves with unusual vigour. "It's just a two-week mooring," I muttered tersely.

"Oh, don't be wet," snapped Nina.

"You've been gone a few days and I was looking forward to showing you the Edge with Eddie." Even as I said it, I realised how sulky and childish I sounded.

"For God's sake. Pour yourself a drink and snap out of it," she replied. "You haven't even asked how the tarot reading went. I'm going to have a shower."

She stomped off to the stern with my traitorous little dog trotting in her wake. I opened a bottle of red, poured myself a generous glass and began to trim the fatty rind off some pork chops. I planned to throw them into a pot with some cider and vegetables but the cosy and intimate evening that I'd envisaged for our reunion had evaporated.

Or had it? Nina seemed in a peace-making mood by the time she returned, flushed from the heat of the shower and with her short hair still wet and tousled. That reminded me, I needed to check the boat's water level. It would be getting low after four days on the mooring. She put a hand on my shoulder. "Sorry, to snap. Bit tired after dealing with Mummy for a couple of days."

"No problem," I said, pouring her a glass of red and topping myself up. "Sorry for acting like a kid. Tell me about the tarot card reading. Full disclosure."

She collapsed into an armchair with her legs tucked sideways and Eddie leapt up onto her lap. "Well, she laid out twelve cards …"

"Same with me," I said, as I ran a peeler along some carrots.

"And she told me all about Alan."

Captain Alan Wilde had been killed during a firefight with the Taliban in Afghanistan. He was just 32 years old, and he had been married to Nina for just six weeks. "That must have been tough," I said sympathetically. I decided not to point out that the whole world knew about Nina and Alan after she prompted headlines in all the national newspapers by going missing immediately after his funeral. It had been her way of dealing with her grief and anger at the time. It would have been easy for Heloise to find this out in advance.

"It was a bit – but it was also comforting in a way. She told me all about Mummy." The formidable Mrs Jill Aston is 73 and living near Salisbury. But then, we had already told Heloise that Nina was visiting her poorly mother. So, perhaps it wasn't surprising that she saw Mrs Aston in the cards.

"Did … er, did she say anything about us?"

"Yes. She said we were very, very close friends who had been through a lot together."

Again, I thought to myself, it wasn't hard to draw this

conclusion after a quick internet search of our names.

"And in the future?" I asked tentatively. I managed to avoid looking at her as I swept the sliced carrots into a pan.

"She said we were set fair," said Nina seriously. "Those were the words she used. Set fair."

I looked up at her. "Is that all?"

"But that's optimistic, isn't it?" said Nina smiling.

"It's a bit vague," I protested, sloshing half a pint of cider into the pan.

"Well, there was a bit more - but not for sharing," said Nina.

"What? That's not fair. I told you everything."

Nina ignored me. "I had a couple of cards which suggested Amsterdam might be on the horizon too – so we need to start planning for that if we're going. Perhaps we can take Eddie if we go by train?"

"That could have been anywhere," I said testily. I was still annoyed by her lack of detail about the future of our relationship. "A place of water, over the water. It could have been the Venetian hotel in Vegas or a waterpark in Dubai!" Nina decided to ignore this too and sipped her wine.

"And she saw me in some kind of dark place too. So, wherever it is, I think we're going to be there together Jack." I bent down to light a ring on the hob with a match and began browning the pork. "In fact, I know we are, and it'll happen very soon."

I looked back at her. "What d'you mean?" I asked suspiciously.

You're going back down the tunnels," she said with a smile. "And this time I'm coming with you!"

"What are you talking about?"

"Finish your cooking and I'll tell you all about it." I quickly tipped some chicken stock, frozen peas and chopped pepper in with the carrots and cider, hurriedly added the chops, covered it all with a lid and went to sit in the chair next to her. "Okay then. The reason I was so long was that Hel has invited us into The Millionaire Tunnels – for a séance!"

"A séance! You've got to be kidding," I said. "They're banned. The tour guide told me."

"Straight up. She's very excited about it. Nick says he can persuade the head of tours to give him the entrance key for an evening. She says they both know a few people who will pay £200 each to be invited. People who want to talk to their dead loved ones." I looked at her and shook my head in disbelief. "She needs the money, Jack. She's got something wrong with her chimney pipe which needs fixing urgently. It's freezing on that boat."

Suddenly, I realised what this was all about. She grimaced as a look of horror came across my face. "That's not why you want to do this, is it?" I asked quietly.

"The tunnels were used for this all the time. They've got quite a reputation," she continued. "It's a very sympathetic place for mediums according to Hel. And I haven't seen them yet. This is my chance. They sound amazing."

"And that's not why you want to go either. It's not, is it?"

She gave me a level look back and bit her lower lip. Then she sighed. "Okay. Alright. Yes. I want to see if I can communicate with Alan through Hel. There. I've said it. Satisfied? There was so much we didn't get to say to each other before he died. It was all so sudden." Nina's big black eyes filled with tears. "I know you'll think it's silly and stupid. But I believe in Hel, and she thinks there's a chance it might work with the right person, and in the right place. That's what we spent so much time talking about this afternoon."

"I can imagine," I said, taking one of her hands in both of mine. "But look Nina. I'm worried this will send you straight back to square one. You've been doing great, but this could reopen a whole new bucket load of grief for you. Who knows what she might say?"

"But Jack, it won't be Hel talking. It will be Alan."

I shook my head fiercely. "That's just crazy."

She rested her other hand on mine. "I love that you are trying to look out for me, Jack. But I have to do this. My mind is made up. If I don't do it, I'll always wonder if I missed my only chance to talk to Alan for one last time. Don't you see that?" I shook my head again. "But I can't do it without you, Jack. I'm asking you to come with us. I'm asking you to be there for me. You will come, won't you?"

"When is this happening?"

"Saturday night. Tomorrow. We'll all meet on Hel's boat at 11 p.m. and walk to the tunnels from there. Please say you'll come with us."

I looked at her hopeful face. I had no faith that this madness would end happily for her – but there was no way I could refuse her plea for help. And someone would need to be there to pick up the pieces. It had to be me.

"Jack?" she whispered. "Will you come with me? Please."

"I'll need to go back to the cashpoint in the morning. I assume it's cash only?" She nodded hopefully. £400?" She nodded again. I blew out my cheeks. "Ok. I don't like it. In fact, I hate it. But I won't let you go on your own."

Eddie leapt to the ground as she stood up quickly and then bent down to give me a tight hug. "Oh, thank you, thank you, thank you, you darling man," she said as she planted a kiss on my lips. It'll be alright. It really will."

I looked at her dubiously but decided not to say anything more. It was just nice to bask in her wholehearted approval for a moment.

CHAPTER 10

Nina and I walked Eddie on Kinver Edge the next morning at her suggestion. She was obviously keen to mend fences for the broken arrangement of the previous day and to say thank you for going along with her mad scheme. Afterwards, we collected our bikes from the little shop off the High Street. They had both been efficiently repaired and serviced. We paused to have coffee in the little bar-café next door, but there was no sign of the Eastern European waiter who had fled from me twice, once at the bar and once, with his family on the Edge. I told Nina about the two incidents, but she was as baffled as me.

We pushed our bikes through town because we still had Eddie with us. But once on the towpath, we let him run free and pedalled slowly along, one behind the other. However, once again, Heloise ambushed us as we were passing her scruffy plant-strewn boat. She rushed out calling "Nina, Nina!" and grabbed Nina's arm as she braked and stopped. "I need to talk to you."

"What is it?" I asked.

"What's wrong?" asked Nina, looking into the young woman's anxious face.

Heloise looked worriedly up and down the canal. "It's Nick. I told him I'd invited you both to the séance and he went mad. I don't understand it. He doesn't want you to come. He says we've got enough people already. He was really angry with me." She was wringing her hands and looking thoroughly miserable.

I looked across at Nina and she too looked crestfallen. One part of me was secretly punching the air in delight. We wouldn't have to go through with this ridiculous farce and risk destabilising her slow recovery – and we would save £400. But the other part of me felt a deep sympathy for Nina's dashed hopes of somehow reconnecting with her dead husband.

"Where is he? Why don't we try to persuade him otherwise," I heard myself saying. The two women looked up at me hopefully.

"Oh, would you? Would you try? I know how much it would mean to Nina," said Heloise.

I realised I was also feeling a perverse sense of bloody-mindedness about the whole situation. I had very little desire to join this ridiculous escapade. But now Nick the Dick was trying to stop me, I felt quite strongly that I wanted to go. Who was he to stop Nina? And why was he throwing his weight around if his girlfriend had already agreed to the arrangement? "Is he on board your boat?"

"No," said Heloise. "He stomped off for a pint at The Anchor." She pointed back down the canal towards Kinver. "It's about three miles that way, at Caunsall. Just before Cookley."

I knew where she meant. I had thought of stopping there for a pint myself on our recent journey. "Alright then," I said to Nina. "You take Eddie on home. I'll go and see if I can persuade him to change his mind."

"I should come with you," said Nina. "I'm sure Hel could look after Eddie for now."

"No," I said firmly. "I know what I have to say, and it'll be easier to say it if you're not there."

Heloise regripped Nina's arm. "Let him go, Nina. I'll walk back to your boat with you and Eddie if you like."

Nina nodded reluctantly and I left both women on the towpath as I cycled off, back the way we had come in the direction of Kinver. I enjoyed the ride. It had been some time since the bikes had been properly roadworthy and the night-time rain and early morning drizzle had given way to bright sunshine which made the trees look even more golden. It was a Saturday and so there were more people about than usual - joggers, dog-walkers, cyclists, and anglers – all getting in each other's way with differing degrees of good humour or frustration. The occasional passing boat also seemed to be more frequent than during the week.

'Life's Better by Water' is the catchphrase of The Canal and River Trust, the organisation which manages the country's navigable waterways. It tries to stress how much happier people are when they're on or alongside the water – but as I cycled along the busy towpath, I reflected again that the CRT has its work cut out trying to referee between so many potential conflicting interests. My time on the canal had already shown me that most liveaboard narrowboaters had little time for the inexperienced holidaymakers who hired their boats. Most anglers seemed to resent the boat traffic which forced them to pull in their lines. Towpath pedestrians were annoyed by cyclists who didn't sound their bells. The cyclists were frustrated by dog walkers whose stretchy leads blocked their progress. And lots of people who lived in homes by the canals seemed to resent the growing number of people who were using them. In short, in spite of the mindfulness being promoted by the CRT, there seemed to be a lot of testiness on the towpath.

The organisation also has a massive job maintaining a 200-year-old network of more than 2,000 miles of canals, rivers, reservoirs and docks out of a declining budget. By and large, I think they do a pretty good job. But judging by posts on social media and the letters pages of the boaters' magazines, plenty of the other 30,000 inland boat owners begged to differ with me.

A fisherman looked up to glare at me as I passed, as if in disagreement with my thoughts. And a few minutes later, a couple with a Jack Russell on a lead tutted when I sounded my bell to warn them of my approach. I often find that I'm castigated as negligent if I don't sound my bell or told off for being too aggressive if I do.

Nevertheless, I made fast progress beyond Kinver and I was soon swinging away from the towpath and crossing a weak road bridge over a pretty stretch of the Stour to enter the little village of Caunsall. The Anchor quickly loomed up on my right-hand side. I chained the bike to an outdoor table and pushed open a narrow front door which led straight into the bar. It was a genuine boozer with no sign of recent prettification by a brewery's design consultants – thank goodness. And it was clearly very popular on a Saturday lunchtime. All of the outside car parking spaces had been filled and the overflow had stretched down the lane. Inside, most of the tables had been taken – including one, by the door, where a man was blissfully asleep and snoring gently, his head tipped back against the wall. A prominent sign at the bar said 'Cash Only' but, conveniently, the owners had installed a cashpoint machine just inside the main bar. I had never seen one inside a pub before and I was impressed by the initiative.

I scanned the room and quickly saw Nick. He was sitting on his own at a corner table. He hadn't seen me yet because his head was bent over a plate full of white rolls on a little round table in front of him. His glass looked as though it was half-full, although in his case, it was probably better described as half-empty. I turned back to the young barmaid. "Two pints of whatever that guy over there is having." I scanned the menu. It was unusual to say the least. I could only choose from three types of bap - pork, beef or cheese. And the choice of salad was to have it or go without. One of the optional extras was an entire jar of shallots in vinegar for £4.50.

I decided to pass on the pickles, ordered two beef baps and told her I'd be sitting with Nick. Then I collected my pints and moved over to his table. "Hi Nick. Mind if I join you?"

He looked up with a jolt and his eyes narrowed as he recognised me. I sat down before he had a chance to reply. "There you go," I said, sliding a full pint glass across the table towards him. "They said you were drinking HPA. Cheers." I took a swallow from my glass and to my astonishment a plate suddenly appeared in front of me. It had taken barely 45 seconds to process my food order. There must have been a mountain of pre-filled baps waiting in the kitchen for instantaneous service.

Nick's food looked more substantial than mine as he'd chosen three baps plus the salad option. The salad consisted of a mound of large, quartered tomatoes next to another mound of very large raw Spanish onions, also quartered, and a pile of sliced cucumber. He was still staring at me as I bit into the bap. The roast beef was thick and tasty. "Mmm…this is very good. Do they roast it on the premises?"

"What are you doing here?" he said.

I took another bite from my bap and held up a finger to ask for his patience while I chewed on it. This made him look very cross. I was starting to enjoy myself. I had a battle plan. But I also knew the old general's view that few plans survive first contact with the enemy. We would have to see about that, wouldn't we?

"Honestly, this is very good. It's a nice fresh roll too. Or is it a bap? What's the difference? Do you know if there's any horseradish?" I asked, looking round. "Ah yes, there it is. Excuse me a minute." I nipped across to a little serving counter which was filled with little plastic bags of assorted sauces. "Mayonnaise, ketchup and mustard too!" I said, returning to my seat. "They think of everything. And it's so reasonably priced. £3 a bap! And no waiting. You can't go wrong, can you? Is this your local then Nick?"

He was still giving me the hard stare and he didn't stop as he took a drink of beer. He wiped his mouth with the back of his hand. "I said, what are you doing here?"

I wiped my mouth with a paper napkin. "Well, you see Nick. I come in peace to sort out a little misunderstanding. Hence the peace offering," I added, indicating his untouched second pint of beer. "On top of the bottle of red wine I brought the other evening. But who's counting, eh? Did you enjoy it? It was quite a good Malbec I seem to remember."

I was happy to hold his stare as he leaned forward and very quietly said, "This is about the séance, isn't it?"

"Yes, Nick. It is about the séance," I replied in an equally quiet voice. "As you know, Hel invited Nina to the fun and games this evening. And Nina has a very particular and personal reason for wanting to go. I'm not sure if Hel told you, but Nina lost her husband a couple of years ago. He was a soldier, an officer fighting in Afghanistan and a bit of a war hero. And Nina is desperate for your girlfriend to try to connect with him, if that's the right word. What is the right word exactly? Reach out to him from beyond the grave? Dial him up? Whatever it is, I think it's probably a load of nonsense, but a deal is a deal and now Hel tells us you don't want Nina to go tonight. So yes, I'm here to discuss this with you."

Nick squared his shoulders and sat up straight. He was muscular with broad shoulders and large biceps. I guessed that he enjoyed looking at himself in a gym mirror. I took another bite from my bap and chewed it while he leaned forward. "Okay listen. You and your girlfriend or whatever she is, aren't coming, alright? We're full. That's all there is to say."

I made him wait for a reply until I had finished my mouthful of beef bap and washed it down with some beer. "But Nick," I said. "Come on. Be reasonable. Why would you turn down an extra £400 for your girlfriend? She obviously needs the cash to spend on her boat before it gets really cold. And there can't be that many people willing to pay that much money to go to a séance – wherever it takes place."

"I don't think you heard me," he said. His lips were barely moving as he spoke. He'd clearly been watching too many old gangster films. "You aren't coming. We're full. Hel should never have asked you and your friend without checking with me first."

"But she did ask Nina, didn't she Nick? And Nina told her we'd both be going. And Hel agreed. And we agreed to pay £400 in cash. So, apart from making the venue available Nick, I'm not sure what this has to do with you."

He narrowed his eyes. "It's got everything to do with me," he said. "It was my idea. I promised Hel we'd raise a grand for her. We have five people coming already. There isn't room for anyone else."

"What d'you mean there isn't room? I've been down those tunnels. I assume you're going to hold the séance in the canteen. Is that right?" He looked surprised. "Yes, I've seen the old candelabras where they used to do this sort of thing. It's a big room. You could take ten or twenty down there if you wanted to."

He continued to give me his hard stare as he put his elbows on the table and rested his chin on his clenched fists. "You aren't coming."

"Final word?"

"Final word."

I wiped my mouth with a paper napkin. "Okay then Nick. Let's just recap, shall we? I've appealed to your sense of justice – because we'd already agreed the deal with Hel. And I've appealed to your sense of charity – because this means a great deal to a lovely woman who was cruelly widowed at a young age. Did I mention that she'd only been married for six weeks? No, I don't think I did. And I've appealed to your sense of generosity – because Hel will get another £400 for her troubles. And still, you're saying no. Is that right?"

"That's right. You aren't coming," he repeated.

"Okay, so now I'm just going to have to appeal to your sense of self-preservation."

He blinked a couple of times – which seemed to me like progress. There was only one way to get through to people like Nick, and that was to threaten their own sense of security. "What d'you mean?"

"Well, you see, if you don't let Hel welcome Nina and me to your séance tonight, in return for £400 cash, I'm just going to have to see who else might be interested in your little arrangement. I don't know who exactly is in charge of the museum, but I'm sure I can quickly find out and I'm equally sure they'd be interested in this cosy little deal between the keyholder and a tour guide, who is also a security officer next door. That's a point. Maybe the people who rent the warehouse next door would also be interested in the extra-curricular money-making activities of one of their employees? And if they're not bothered, perhaps the police might be. Surely, this would be classed as trespass or breaking and entering, wouldn't it? Is there a police station in Kinver? No, Wolverhampton would be the closest, I suppose. And, in the unlikely case that none of those people are bothered,

I can absolutely guarantee the intense interest of the local press or maybe, even the national newspapers. Probably TV and radio too. They'd love a story like this. Believe me, I would know. I'm a journalist by the way."

I sat back, finished my pint and pushed his full pint glass towards him. "So, Nick. D'you want to risk me spending the afternoon trying to do any of those things? Because I can do all of that, you know? I'm a fast worker when I need to be. Do you want to risk going ahead and finding a reception committee waiting for you tonight? Either the police, or your bosses, or His Majesty's press and media? Or do you just want to cancel the idea altogether, which means sacrificing all of that money for Hel – and disappointing the others who have been invited? Or do you just want to invite two more people – me and Nina - and avoid all of that unnecessary fuss and embarrassment?"

To say someone looks like 'they're swallowing a wasp' is a terrible cliché and an image I could never really picture until that moment. But Nick's facial self-control underwent severe challenges. His lips had pursed, his jaw muscles clenched and unclenched, and I swear he went cross-eyed at one point. Finally, in a slightly hoarse voice he whispered, "The woman can come. But not you."

I shook my head. "Sorry Nick. Not good enough. This is going to be a very emotional experience for my friend. I've promised I shall be there for her, and I intend to keep that promise – if it all goes ahead of course …"

"It's going ahead," he said with grim determination.

"Fine. Then you've got two more people coming, haven't you? Just as Hel agreed." He couldn't bring himself to speak. Eventually, he just nodded slowly, with hatred in his eyes.

"Excellent. I knew we could do business." I stood up and held out a hand which he ignored. "Right then. See you at Magic Meg at 11 p.m. Don't go without us, will you? You know what'll happen if you do."

"Just fuck off," he growled. I almost felt a pang of sympathy for him. Almost, though not quite.

"Enjoy your pint." I picked up my uneaten bap, made for the door and ate it happily as I cycled, one-handed, back to our mooring.

CHAPTER 11

I stopped at Magic Meg in case Nina had remained with Heloise and sure enough, Nina's bike was on the stern tiller platform and Eddie barked as soon as I called out. My little dog bounded out to say hello followed by the two women.

"How did you get on?" asked Nina anxiously.

"Did you find Nick?"

"Yes. I found him in The Anchor. We chatted it through over a pint and he's changed his mind. He says it's fine for me and Nina to come tonight. We'll meet you here at 11 o'clock as arranged." I tried very hard not to look smug, but probably failed.

Heloise looked genuinely shocked. "Really? Are you sure? Nick doesn't change his mind very easily."

I smiled at her. "I'm sure he doesn't. I won't pretend he's overjoyed about it – but he's accepted that we're coming."

Nina was smiling broadly at my news. "Oh, well done Jack!" She skipped across the towpath and gave me a kiss on the cheek.

'All hail the conquering hero', I thought to myself with satisfaction. "Come on. Fetch your bike. We'll get back to our boat now." The two women embraced even more affectionately than before, and Heloise watched us cycle away with Eddie in the vanguard.

Nina quickly pedalled up alongside me. "How did you do it?"

"I tried being nice. I even bought him a drink. But that didn't work. So, I blackmailed him."

"What? How? What did you say to him?"

"I just told him to honour the deal you made with Hel or I'd reveal his little money-making scheme to his bosses, or the police, or the media – or all three."

"Jack!"

I gave her the best shrug that you can whilst riding a bike. "He's a piece of work. It was the only way to get through to Nasty Nick in the end."

"But did he say why he didn't want us to come?" asked Nina.

"No. That's what's so strange. You think he'd be happy with another four hundred quid for Hel. And I'm sure he'll be taking a hefty cut too. But no. All he kept saying was that they couldn't take any more people. Obviously, he doesn't like me. But even so. Maybe he just doesn't like his girlfriend making decisions without his agreement."

"I'm sure he's very controlling," said Nina. "I did try to suggest to Hel that he might be gaslighting her." We slipped into single file to pass another scowling fisherman. "He does sound a bit of a bully," she said as she returned to a position alongside me.

I looked up to see Eddie sprinting back towards us in some distress. His tail was firmly tucked between his legs and his ears were flat and pointing backwards. He stopped every few metres to paw his nose. "What's wrong with him?" said Nina in a panicked voice.

We both dismounted quickly and knelt down to check him over. I couldn't see anything but guessed the problem. "It's that bloody hornet's nest. It's just up ahead, isn't it? He must have put his nose into the hollow of the tree."

"Oh, you poor, poor darling," said Nina, kissing him on the top of his head. Eddie was still trying to wipe the pain away from his snout. I picked him up and tried to carry him as I wheeled my bike, but he's deceptively heavy for a little dog and I was soon forced to return him to the ground. He seemed to be walking okay now, but he had the sense to trot quickly past the hollow in the tree with a rueful glance. He had stopped pausing to rub his nose by the time we reached Jumping Jack Flash where we examined him more closely. There was no sign of a sting or a wound and he just seemed sorry for himself rather than badly hurt. I fetched him a dried pig's ear from his treat drawer, and he took it to his basket where he hid it under his soft bedding.

We decided to stay with Eddie for a lazy afternoon on the boat. Nina had him on her lap while I idly surfed the internet on my laptop. "Did I tell you I paddled over for a closer look at The Devil's Den?" I asked Nina as she got up to make a pot of tea. I told her about how I hired the dinghy which belonged to the two young men – although I neglected to tell her about the paintball gun. "Pearson's say it was a boathouse used by the Foley family of Prestwood Hall. That seems to make sense." I did a bit more online searching and found a local newspaper article which referred to a row over the man-made cave between various boating groups and British Waterways, the organisation which preceded the Canal and Rivers Trust. It seemed that British Waterways had installed the oak door with a small gap at the top to protect a bat colony in the boathouse and to make it safe.

However, the treasurer of the Staffs & Worcs Canal Society fumed: "*As far as we know, the boathouse is a unique structure of the waterways and certainly an historic feature of our canal. We have had a lot of feedback from our 400 members who are outraged that something that has been here for 200 years has had a nasty wooden door plonked across it.*"

But a British Waterways official hit back. "*The cave was clearly showing signs of anti-social behaviour with discarded cans and bottles and drug paraphernalia. With the only access to the cave by a steep cliff above or by water, any attempts to enter could pose serious safety risks.*"

"So, health and safety won the day," observed Nina. "And the door remained in place."

"And the bats stayed undisturbed," I added.

The article went on to say the boathouse was carved out of the rock in about 1770, at the same time as the canal was being built through the Prestwood Hall estate. The Foley ironmasters owned the estate at the time and insisted on its construction as part of the price for crossing their land.

I opened up another tab and typed Prestwood Hall. An old black and white engraving of an impressive Gothic mansion appeared.

However, the accompanying text told me it had been demolished in 1921 after a disastrous fire. A tuberculosis sanatorium had been built on the site and it was now owned by a nursing home company.

"So, The Devil's Den is now owned by a care home," said Nina. "How very prosaic."

"The Foleys must have been incredibly rich in their day," I replied. I spent another half-hour on the search engine and discovered that the family and their descendants also owned Stourton Castle, an old royal hunting lodge that was very close to our mooring as well as Dunsley Hall, a 13th century manor house that was now operating as a four-star hotel. So, all three local mansions – Prestwood Hall, Stourton Castle and Dunsley Hall had been lived in by the Foleys and all three were easily within a one-mile radius of The Devil's Den and our mooring. It made me wonder whether any kind of tunnel had been excavated to link the boathouse with one of the family's grand homes. Prestwood Hall had been demolished and Stourton Castle was now a complex of private apartments and smaller homes.

"I think we'll eat out tonight," I said. "I'd like to see Dunsley Hall Hotel. It's just back along the canal near Dunsley Tunnel."

It was about seven o'clock when we walked up to the hotel, with our torches showing the way. The main house, which hosted the hotel, was an impressive red brick edifice with gable ends and towering chimneys. I had hoped to have a good look inside, but the main restaurant was a smokehouse in a modern-looking building across a courtyard from the hotel. A table of menus in the reception area of the restaurant was decorated with a mannikin dressed as a witch and covered in fake cobwebs out of a spray can.

"Hallowe'en," I muttered. "It's such a stupid American import. I hate it. All that plastic tat and trick or treating. It just teaches kids how to beg."

"Mr Grumpy speaks," said Nina.

"It's true," I protested as we sat down at a window table. "People spend all their time talking to kids about stranger-danger and then send them to knock on strangers' doors and ask for sweets!" I scanned the menu. There were lots of barbecue smoked meat dishes. "And horror films. God, how I hate horror films. What a waste of time. I'm always left wondering at the sheer stupidity of the characters. There's always a moment when you're shouting at the screen as they decide to go camping in the woods at night or open the door to wander around some ruined old mansion."

"But if they didn't do that, there wouldn't be a film," Nina protested with a laugh.

"Precisely, the whole premise is flawed. In real life, people wouldn't do those things. They'd run a mile." We agreed to split a bottle of red and ordered some chicken wing starters and steaks.

"Well, if this was a Hallowe'en horror film, I suppose you'd be shouting at us not to go down the tunnels for a séance tonight?" said Nina.

"Damn right I would. It's a bloody stupid idea."

"And yet, you persuaded Nick to let us go."

"Yes. Because you've set your heart on it. But I still think it's daft."

"Well, you don't have to come," she said crossly, folding her arms.

"You said you wanted me to come and I'm coming," I replied firmly. "And I'm paying £200 for the privilege. Although frankly, I think you should pay for me and I'm definitely not paying for you."

"We can each pay for ourselves," she said. I recognised the stubborn set of her jaw only too well. "But you can pay for dinner because this place was your idea."

"Actually, it's got quite a grisly history," I said. "It's a shame the restaurant isn't in the main house. I'd have liked to have seen it. It was the home of someone called Ben Robins who was murdered in 1812. His killer was encased in irons on a gibbet in Gibbet Wood, which is somewhere near here. Apparently, his widow couldn't bear to see the place out of her window in the house, so she had it bricked up."

Nina shook her head at me. "How do you come up with this

stuff?" she asked.

"There you go," said a waitress. She was dressed as some kind of pixie. "And later, if you're interested, the chef has a special choice of Hallowe'en desserts. There's Zombie Brain Cupcakes or a coffin-shaped chocolate fudge cake. Or there's tombstone cookies and witches' brew ice cream. And we've got ..."

Nina broke in hurriedly. My head had tipped backwards and my eyes were rolling upwards. "That's alright thanks. I'm sorry," she said. She nodded across at me. "He doesn't do Hallowe'en. But he does like spirits."

CHAPTER 12

I might not do Hallowe'en, but I still found myself going to an underground séance in walking boots and warm clothing a few hours later. Nick opened the stern doors on Magic Meg. He gave me a hard look, which I was now very familiar with, and grudgingly backed away so we could descend into the interior. We switched off our torches and Heloise introduced us to a middle-aged couple who were seated at the table.

"Richard and Joyce, this is Jack and Nina. Richard and Joyce are regular clients of mine," she explained. "I read their tarot cards once a month."

The couple looked as though they were in their mid to late sixties. He was bald and careworn while she was plump with metal glasses and grey hair.

"How do," said Richard.

"Pleased to meet you," said Joyce.

"Likewise," said Nina politely. We all shook hands. We could have been greeting each other at the start of a dinner party rather than an underground spectral expedition.

"Have you got Hel's money?" asked Nick with a distinct lack of grace. Nina and I both pulled out four fifty-pound notes and put them in a biscuit tin he was holding. Richard and Joyce had already deposited their cash into it. Then he looped the straps of a big canvas bag over one shoulder and picked up a torch. "Right then, let's go," he said.

"Is this everyone," I asked in surprise. Nick had made a big thing about there being no room for Nina and me to join the party.

"There are another three joining us," said Heloise as she

adjusted her own shoulder bag. "They'll meet us near the entrance to the tunnel."

I thought this was a slightly strange arrangement, but we all fell into step for the fifteen-minute walk to the museum entrance of The Millionaire Tunnels. I found myself walking alongside Joyce. Nina and Richard were behind us and Nick and Heloise took the lead.

"This is exciting, isn't it?" whispered Joyce. "Although I am a bit nervous." I detected a hint of a Geordie accent.

"I'm sure it will be fine," I said quietly to her.

"Who do you want to contact if you don't mind me asking?" she continued. She was breathing quite heavily now as Nick was setting a decent pace.

"I don't want to contact anyone," I said. "I'm just keeping Nina company. She wants to hear from her husband." I shook my head to myself in the dark. Just saying this out loud seemed like lunacy. "What about you?"

"Oh. We lost our daughter when she was little. It was a heart condition. She was our only child. Her name was Annie. We'd love to know that she's okay."

Apart from being dead, I thought to myself. I didn't doubt Heloise's genuine belief in her psychic gifts, but was it right to exploit a parent's lifelong grief in this way? "I'm sorry," I said inadequately.

We continued our quiet conversation although at one point Joyce stopped to complain about a stitch. I asked Nick to slow down and was rewarded with a scowl. Joyce told me that the couple lived in a bungalow in Kidderminster and that her husband Richard was now retired from his job as a car mechanic. She admitted that they struggled to make ends meet on their modest pensions, but they found their monthly sessions with Heloise a great comfort. They had both been 'a bit poorly' recently. Richard had undergone knee surgery and Joyce had a stent fitted after a heart attack. "I've got so many tablets to take now, it's a wonder I don't rattle when I walk," she told me. I made some sympathetic noises but quietly wondered to myself whether this night-time escapade was a good idea for someone with a heart condition.

Eventually, we were skirting the outer perimeter fence of the tunnel complex and stopped about twenty metres from the entrance gate into the museum's car-parking area. I checked my watch. Twenty past eleven. I could just about see along the approachway which had been carved into the hill and which led to the tunnel's entrance. At the end, a dim yellow light shone above the metal door I had entered for the tour.

"Turn off your torches and just wait here," Nick ordered brusquely. Then he walked a short way back along the road and began speaking to someone on his mobile. An owl began hooting from somewhere on the rising land above us and the sky lightened slightly as a half-moon emerged from behind some cloud. A few moments later, the headlights of a car appeared and slowed to a stop next to Nick. The car's engine stayed on and steam from its exhaust rose into the cold night air. I watched Nick bend down and speak to the driver who passed something to him. Nick passed something back to him in return. Then the car moved away and Nick rejoined us with a bunch of keys visible in one hand. I assumed the head of tours had just dropped by.

"What now?" I asked.

Nick's eyes were still distinctly unfriendly below his dark woollen hat. "We wait a bit longer," he said.

"Brrr…it's a bit parky standing around here," said Richard. Everyone ignored him except Joyce who wrapped an arm around his waist. We all lapsed into silence.

A few minutes later another car appeared. A silver estate car. This one stopped and also kept its engine running. Nick moved across and opened the nearside rear door. A man got out just as another two emerged from the far side of the vehicle. They gathered together and began walking towards us. I realised with a jolt of surprise that I knew who these men were. I couldn't see their faces, but I could see their distinctive silhouettes in the lights of the car's headlamps. One was fat, one was short, and one was tall. It was Boggis and Bunce and Bean! The car, which I saw now was a taxi, moved off.

Nina must have heard my sharp intake of breath. "What is it?" she whispered.

"These guys were on the tunnel tour with me," I said quietly.

She shrugged. She was probably right. After all, I had also been on the tunnel tour, and I now found myself in the same place as them. We automatically gathered in a semi-circle facing Nick. He didn't bother with any more introductions, although I could tell the newcomers were checking us out with sidelong glances.

"Okay, listen up," he said in a low voice. "I'll unlock the car park gate in a minute. There's one camera above the door at the entrance which points back towards the fence. We'll be fine if we stay right over on the left-hand side until we get to the end, and then we walk under it to the door. Follow me closely in single file. Got it?" Everyone nodded. "Well go on then," he hissed. "Get into a line."

We strung out behind Nick and followed him to the gate where he fiddled with a padlock, swung one side open slightly, ushered us through and relocked it. We trooped after him, like a crocodile of obedient schoolchildren, along the left-hand side of the approach way to the tunnel entrance. I looked across at the CCTV camera mounted above the light above the door. It did look as though it was tilted forward and sideways too much to be fully effective. Had Nick or someone helpfully meddled with it to create a blind spot?

Our route clung closely to the front of the big tunnel entrance until Nick reached the heavy metal door which he opened with two more keys. We entered one by one and waited on the other side as he closed and locked it again. "Okay, you can use your torches now," he said. "Stay close together and follow me."

There were now nine of us in total. Nick and Heloise, me and Nina, Richard and Joyce and Boggis, Bunce and Bean. Our combined torch power provided plenty of light for our brief journey to the canteen. There was barely any sound apart from our shoes scraping on the sandstone floor and Joyce's heavy breathing. She had an arm linked through Richard's, but she had clearly found the effort of the walk or the excitement of the night-time trespass a bit much.

Nick swung his bag onto the canteen's shiny metal serving counter and indicated that Boggis should help him carry a square metal table into the centre of the large room. Then he scraped four rusting chairs up to the table before dipping into his bag and retrieving a small plastic supermarket bag. We all shone our torches on him as he carried this across to the table, stepped onto it via a chair and carefully placed eight tea-tree lights on the candelabra above it. He lit them with a cigarette lighter and jumped back onto the floor. A small pool of flickering light now faintly illuminated the table.

Heloise began to move towards his bag, but he snapped at her. "I'll do it." He moved fast, back towards the counter and extracted a tube of rolled up paper and a flat heart-shaped piece of glass which he laid on the table. Heloise took one of the seats and spread the paper flat. She weighted each corner with a coin. I could see that the piece of glass had two brass castor wheels on it and a pencil was also secured in place at the point of the heart-shape. She moved the contraption slightly and everyone could see through the glass that the pencil had made a mark on the paper.

"Ready?" asked Nick. She nodded up at him. "Okay, torches off," he ordered. We all did as we were told and the room was plunged into gloom except for the naked flames flickering above our heads.

"Does it have to be so dark?" asked Joyce nervously.

"The spirits of the dead reside within the realm of darkness and shadow," said Heloise. "The absence of light is essential if we are to invoke them. Please come and sit-down Joyce. And you Richard. And you Nina." They did as they were told, with the couple sitting to either side of Heloise and Nina sitting opposite. "This is a planchette," she said, indicating the heart-shaped piece of glass. "The spirits will guide it if they want to communicate with us." She paused and looked around the table.

"Alright. Place your fore-fingers on the planchette alongside mine please." She had her eyes closed now, but there was no indication that she was in any kind of trance. Her voice was calm and level and pleasant. "I have Richard and Joyce here and they are very anxious for any information about their little girl Annie. And I have Nina here. She wants to contact her husband, Captain Alan Wilde. Is there a spirit here who can help us?"

The room was completely silent now. Everyone was motionless. The flames in the candelabra had settled down and now they were barely flickering at all. I discovered that I was holding my breath. Waiting. Waiting for what? This was all complete nonsense. And yet there was something powerful and strange about the atmosphere around us. I sensed the earth pressing down above us and I also felt the presence of all the thousands of lives that had lived and worked in these tunnels ever since they had been built - and the handful of lives that had ended in them too.

And then it happened. The flat piece of glass started to move about in tiny jerking motions. Joyce gave a little yelp of surprise. There was a small scratching sound. We all leaned forward to try to make out the pencil's markings on the paper. Heloise's eyes were open now and she was staring at the emerging markings. The pencil swooped up in a long curve which curled over at the top before rising again to swoop downwards in another long curve which met the start of the drawing. It looked like it was a picture of a heart, mirroring the heart shape of the planchette.

Then the pencil jerked across to the centre of the heart and began to form words in joined-up writing.

GilbertandLizzy

"Gilbert and Lizzy," said Heloise. "And a heart. Are you Gilbert or Lizzy? Were you sweethearts?" The pencil began moving straight away. It drew a circle around Gilbert before moving on to trace the shape of the heart again. "You are Gilbert and you loved Lizzy.

Is there anything else you want to tell us Gilbert?"

This time, the pencil traced a line outside the heart and began writing again.

IamsorryJack

"I am sorry Jack," read Heloise. I jumped as she read out my name. "There is a Jack here with us tonight Gilbert. He's called Jack Johnson. Are you trying to contact him?" Nina looked up at me from the table, but the pencil moved again briefly.

No

I began to breathe again. "Alright Gilbert. I shall ask you once again. Do you think you can help Richard and Joyce speak to their daughter Annie? It would be very nice of you to try to do this Gilbert." The pencil slowly circled the previous reply and stopped. I saw a single tear sliding down Joyce's flushed cheek. "Alright Gilbert. That's okay. Is there anything anyone would like to ask Gilbert?" she said, looking up and around us all.

"Ask him why he's here," I said quietly.

Heloise looked at me and nodded. She slid the top piece of paper away and let it fall to the floor so that the planchette was resting on a new blank sheet. "Jack wants to know why you are here Gilbert. Why are you in the tunnels?"

GetOutNow

The writing was larger this time and it sat there, a stark warning in the centre of the sheet of paper. "Get out now," read Heloise. "You want us to leave Gilbert? Why do you want us to leave?"

But this time there was no scribbled answer. Because this time, there was the clunk of some kind of metal switch and the room was bathed in electric light. It was blinding at first. We were all blinking or rubbing our eyes and trying to look around us. Who had turned the lights on? The answer quickly became clear. Nick was standing in the corner of the room next to a large electric box mounted on the wall. He must have pulled the lever on its side. But that wasn't what I noticed first. No, what I noticed first was the shotgun he had cradled in his other arm.

"Okay folks. Sorry about this, but the show is over," he said.

Heloise was standing and staring at him. "What the hell, Nick?"

He laughed nastily. "What the hell, Hel?" He nodded to the little man I called Bunce who scurried over to the shoulder bag on the counter and pulled out another shotgun and a pistol. He gave the pistol to Bean who held it level in his long bony fingers and casually pointed it directly at me.

"What are you doing? What's all this about?" asked Heloise again. "Why have you got guns for God's sake?"

"Ah Hel. Don't be like that. In fact, I'm surprised you need to ask me. You're a fortune teller aren't you? I thought you'd know all about this already." He snickered to himself. "No-one will get hurt if everyone does what I say."

The small guy, who looked like a jockey, had positioned himself in the main doorway to the canteen and was holding the shotgun horizontal. Nick was still standing at the counter end of the room and the tall man with the pistol was closest to us. None of them were in the others' firing line which suggested to me that they knew what they were doing. The fattest of the three, Boggis, was leaning against a wall and cleaning his fingernails with the point of a dangerous looking knife.

Richard moved to stand behind Joyce who remained sitting. Her face was rigid with fear and she had turned an unhealthy shade of grey. Nina rose to her feet and stood alongside me. I had plenty of direct experience of her uncanny calmness during stressful situations, but she was holding tightly to my arm.

Heloise looked around the room at all of us and then back at her boyfriend. It was clear she really didn't have a clue what was happening. She went to move towards Nick, but he casually raised the shotgun's two barrels and snapped, "Stay there Hel, there's a good girl."

She stopped and stood still. Her face was transfixed in a combination of shock, fear and fury. "For Christ's sake Nick, what's this all about? This was all your bloody idea in the first place. And who are these jokers? You said they were mates from the pub. Wait. Is this why you didn't want Jack and Nina to come?"

Nick closed his eyes and sighed. "You do drone on. I'm sorry Hel. It was nice while it lasted but I'll be moving on after tonight. Just do exactly as you're told, and it'll all become clear."

"If he won't tell you, I'll have a go," I said. And everyone's heads turned towards me.

CHAPTER 13

"Nick isn't here for the séance and nor are his three chums," I said. "That was just a ruse to borrow the keys and get into the museum tunnels. No, I suspect the real reason is next door, in the warehouse. That's where thirty-two million pounds worth of silver ingots are being stored. They were salvaged from the seabed of the Indian Ocean by a Brit. I don't know how they plan to get in there because it's all sealed off. And I have no idea how they'll manage to take away sixty tonnes of the stuff. But Nick here is a security guard, so he'll know his way around and he'll have a plan. I imagine it's destined for South Africa, which is where these other guys come from."

Boggis, Bunce and Bean all looked at each other when I said this. "Yes, I know you've all been very careful not to say anything so far this evening. That's probably why you didn't meet us on the boat. But you were on the tunnel tour with me, and I heard your accent when you took the selfie. The South African government is trying to claim the silver in the courts. Maybe this is its insurance policy? I don't know if you're spies or crooks, but you've recruited Nick here to help you. I hope they're paying you well, Nick. Are you getting a percentage? I suppose this is why you didn't want me and Nina to come along. You didn't want any more civilians than strictly necessary, did you? But when I threatened to reveal your little escapade, you had no choice did you? You were forced to let us come along. I could have wrecked the whole thing for you, couldn't I Nick?"

Nick walked casually towards me. I braced myself for a physical attack, but I was still surprised when he swung his gun around at the last second and drove the wooden butt hard into my midriff. Every last bit of energy drained out of me as I doubled over and fell to my knees. The nausea and pain were overwhelming. The cramp in my ribs made it almost impossible to breath and I retched to take in oxygen. I looked up at him. Now he had the gun raised vertically in both hands and looked poised to smash the butt down onto my head.

"Leave him alone!" It was Nina. She had moved quickly and was now standing between me and my attacker. Her voice was shaking with emotion.

"You've got a big mouth," said Nick grimly. "And I wouldn't mind shutting it once and for all. I don't like you. Open it once more and you won't leave these tunnels alive, and neither will your girlfriend here. D'you understand?"

I was still struggling to breathe, and my eyes were watering badly, but I nodded up at him. He moved past me to the table where Richard and Joyce had been watching with saucer-like eyes. They both appeared to be shrivelled up, as though trying to make themselves as small and inconspicuous as possible. Nick put a finger on the glass planchette and gave it a flick which sent it rolling off the table and on to the stone floor where it smashed to pieces. Then he looked at his watch.

"Right. Get up." Richard and Joyce rose to their feet quickly while Nina put a hand in my armpit and hauled me up from the floor. "This way. All of you." He headed off with the rest of us following and the gang-of-three picking up the rear. We all relied on our torches once we were out of the canteen, but we hadn't gone far before we stopped again.

"It's here," said Nick, shining his torch at the roof. I recognised the spot immediately. The tour guide had stopped here to talk about the three different types of air-flow systems and how they had evolved over the years. So that was why the South African had taken his selfie! He had angled the camera low down so that his picture captured the two round pipes and the latest square stainless-steel ducting. I began to guess what their plan was.

"You five, sit down there," ordered Nick, "And you watch them," he said to the tall thin man with the pistol. We sat directly on the floor and leaned back against the tunnel wall. My stomach was still gripped in pain, but my breathing was improving as my diaphragm slowly returned to normal.

It must have taken about thirty minutes for Nick and the two others to drag an old metal stepladder to the spot and use some adjustable spanners from Nick's bag to unscrew a bracket which suspended the ducting from the ceiling. Behind the bracket were more bolts holding two sections together which they undid. They pulled one end to the floor and reaffixed the remaining section to the ceiling. They had opened up a man-sized route from the museum into the warehouse. But how would they emerge from it on the other side? The answer to that quickly became clear as Nick dipped his hand back into the bag and pulled out an angle-grinder. It must have been battery driven as he pressed the trigger and it burst into life. The little cutting wheel spun furiously for a few seconds. He gave it to the small man who I'd named Bean and fished out two more replacement batteries and a pack of substitute wheel blades. "They're all charged up. You know what to do. Down to the first junction and ten metres along to the right. I'll be behind you with the torch."

Both men climbed up and disappeared along the ducting. Boggis had been holding the ladder steady for them, but Bean didn't take his eyes off us or lower his pistol for one moment. A short while later we heard the high-pitched whine of the little machine as it sliced through the metal. They must have crawled somewhere on the other side of the new walls that separated the museum from the warehouse.

"How are you?" whispered Nina out of the corner of her mouth. She probably thought the noise of the angle-grinder being funnelled back down the duct would cover her.

"Thanks for stepping in," I whispered back.

But our guard was instantly on the alert. "Be quiet," he snapped. Definitely South African, I thought to myself.

I shifted my backside slightly in an attempt to get more comfortable on the cold floor and felt my phone in a rear trouser pocket. Even if I managed to slip away, I knew it would be useless as a way of raising the alarm. There was no signal of any kind in the tunnels. Our guards knew it too, or they would have taken them off us.

Eventually, after approximately another thirty minutes, the noise stopped and Nick's face appeared above us. He turned full circle and descended backwards on the stepladder. "Okay," he said to the other two. "We're through. Get them lined up." It quickly became clear that we were going to be forced to crawl into the warehouse. I was puzzled. Why not just leave us behind now? We were locked-in and Nick had the only set of keys. Perhaps they wanted to keep us under observation and didn't want to split their manpower.

Nick disappeared again and the barrel of the pistol waved me up first. There was just enough room to crawl along the square metal tunnel and Nick's torch was shining into my eyes as I moved towards him. He had tucked himself into the left-hand side of a T-junction and when I reached him, he tersely told me to go right. A little way ahead, another torch light was shining upwards and reflecting off the shiny surfaces. As I got nearer, I saw a coffin-sized piece of metal had been neatly cut out of the right-hand side of the ducting and the little man's head was poking through it. He must be standing on another stepladder. I looked backwards. Nina was inching towards me, and I could just make out Heloise behind her. They were leaving Richard and Joyce until last. I imagined that Joyce would find it all a bit of a struggle.

"Come down here," Bunce ordered from below.

I gingerly felt the freshly cut edge of the metal. It was okay. They had left the bottom of their cut-out intact and simply pushed it out and folded it over. I flopped onto my belly with my legs dangling out and felt two hands grab my feet and guide them onto the ladder. There was a moment, when I had descended, that I contemplated trying to overpower the man or flee while he was preoccupied with the others. But then what? The rest weren't far away, and I didn't fancy my chances.

Blundering around in pitch darkness and being chased by men with torches and guns didn't sound sensible.

The moment passed and we were soon all gathered together, although Joyce needed her husband, Nina and me to help her descend the stepladder with much huffing and puffing. Her shoulders were heaving and she was weeping silently on Richard's shoulder by the time Nick dropped to the floor. His shotgun had been strapped to his back, but he loosened it now and crooked it under one arm. His other hand still held a torch.

"Follow me and stick together," he ordered. "Watch them," he told his co-conspirators. It was interesting, I thought, as we began to make our way along a lengthy connecting tunnel. It did seem as though Nick was firmly in charge of the operation. Clearly, he had the inside knowledge to come up with the plan – both as a museum tour guide and a security guard at the warehouse. But if the others were experienced South African agents of some kind, I would have expected them to be a bit more commanding or assertive. Instead, they were just efficiently following his orders. Maybe this was just some kind of old-fashioned criminal heist after all? Or maybe they were all just very self-disciplined?

And what was going through Heloise's head at the moment? She was walking in the line somewhere behind me. I tried to imagine her shock at the scale of Nick's betrayal and her guilt at leading her four 'clients' into this mess. He had exploited her genuine belief in her powers and used her to a degree that was truly evil. The poor wretched girl. I vowed to myself that I would make him regret his actions if I possibly could.

We traipsed on by torchlight until we emerged into a much larger space. Nick's torch shone upwards briefly and I saw the roof was significantly higher than it had been. This must be one of the four main tunnels which travelled east to west. We turned left and stayed close to the left-hand wall as we began to make our way along it. Only our guards carried torches now and the beam of one swung off to the right. I was amazed to see an enormous artic lorry parked there, in the centre of the tunnel.

Shortly afterwards, a second emerged from the gloom, parked directly behind the first. I looked at my watch. The luminous hands told me it was now 1.30 a.m.

We were motioned to stop immediately after passing the lorries. It looked as though a side tunnel had been bricked up although there was a metal door in the centre of the arch. Nick fiddled with a key and kicked it open. It swung sharply inwards with a loud clang.

CHAPTER 14

I peered over his shoulder as he switched on the lights. It was a dormitory. Rusting metal beds stretched away down both sides of a room which had been converted out of a smaller tunnel. And on each of the beds, slowly sitting up and rubbing their eyes, were people. We all filed behind Nick, into the central aisle between the beds. I stared at the beds' occupants, and they stared back at us. None of them moved to get up. "What is this?" asked Nina in a shocked voice by my side.

I counted the beds along one side. There were twenty of them. That meant forty people were down here, sleeping underground. The air was fetid with unwashed body odour. I looked closer. Almost all of the beds seemed to be occupied by men of all ages – from spotty looking teenagers to a few who looked to be in their fifties or sixties. Their hair was exclusively black and most of them had closely cut beards or stubble. There were a couple of women too, pulling shawls around their shoulders and over their heads as they sat up to see who had come into their communal sleeping room.

"Agimor, come here," Nick said to a large man in a bed next to him. The man was bare-chested and looked strong. He got out of bed and padded up to Nick wearing only a pair of shorts. They shook hands. "Agimor, I need you to do a loading job. Tell them all to get dressed and I will fetch you in ten minutes."

The man called Agimor nodded and spoke to everyone in the dormitory in a foreign language. There was a collective groan and muttering when he finished. "BE QUIET,' Nick shouted, and a hush quickly descended. "Ten minutes," he ordered, holding up ten fingers. Then he turned on his heel and marched out of the door with Bunce, Boggis and Bean in close attendance. The door was slammed and a key was turned in the lock.

Agimor rubbed the tightly curled mat of hair on his chest. He said something else to the others in the room which prompted most of them to get out of bed immediately and start putting clothes on. Then he walked towards us, stopped and examined each of us in turn. He smiled and pointed at Heloise. "You are … uh, a pretty lady." Then he pointed at Nina. "And you …" He waved one hand around the room. "We have no more beds. Maybe you have to sleep with Agimor eh?" He gave a deep roar of laughter and cupped one hand over his groin.

"In your dreams, buster," said Nina angrily.

He frowned. "What do you say? Who are you? Why are you here?"

I stepped forward. "We are prisoners of the men outside. The men with guns." I mimed a cocked pistol with my hand. "Who are you? Why are you living down here? Are you prisoners too?"

"Prisoners? Pah," he spat. "We are not prisoners. We pay good money. We come from Albania. I must put on clothes for work." He turned to walk back to his bed where he pulled a cheap-looking suitcase out from underneath.

"Illegal immigrants," I said to Nina. "They must have been smuggled here somehow."

"That explains the East European you frightened when you mentioned the tunnels," she replied. "He probably lived down here at some point and was scared you were onto him."

Of course. That explained it. He must have been smuggled into the country too, along with his wife and child., and been released into the local area to find work and a place to stay. He was probably still paying his debts to whichever criminal gang of traffickers was behind all this. No wonder he had been terrified. He probably thought I was some kind of immigration officer on his trail.

Richard came across to me and whispered in my ear. Both he and Joyce needed to use a lavatory. I told them to come with me and we approached Agimor again. He was lacing up a pair of grubby trainers, but he pointed to a door at the end of the dormitory and the couple scuttled off.

Heloise wandered sadly over to stand with Nina and me. "How are you Hel?" I asked her. Nina rubbed her arm sympathetically.

"It's like some kind of nightmare," she said. "I keep hoping I might wake up in a moment." She stared past me at the two lines of people stretching, yawning and shuffling into their clothes. "Nick must have known these people were down here all of the time that I've known him. He wasn't just keeping people out of the warehouse. He was keeping people in as well." She shuddered, crossed her arms and wrapped both hands around her shoulders. "How could he do that? I feel sick that we …that we were together. And then he used me to betray you. I feel so ashamed. I'm so sorry." Nina folded Heloise into her arms and tried to soothe her. "I thought he was genuinely trying to raise some money for me and my boat. What an idiot I've been."

I held her upper arm. "None of this is your fault," I told her. "He's a nasty bastard and he took you for a ride. You couldn't do much about that, could you?" She shook her head reluctantly. "But I think he may be playing a very risky game."

Nina looked up. "What do you mean?"

"Well, I've been thinking about it. We've got to assume the owners of this warehouse know about all of this haven't we?" I gestured at the beds. "They'll be taking their cut for providing the temporary accommodation, won't they? Maybe they're even the ones who are running the trade."

"Maybe," nodded Nina.

"So, they're also the ones who've got £32 million worth of silver in storage. I don't imagine they'll be too pleased when Nick helps himself to it. I wouldn't fancy having the organised crime gangs of Albania on my trail – not even for that much money."

"Unless …," said Nina thoughtfully, "unless it's a fake heist."

"What do you mean?"

"I mean what if he's been told to do this? He steals the silver. Somehow, the Albanians get to cash it in, and the owner gets an insurance pay out."

"It's a possibility," I said. "But then why go to all the trouble of breaking in from the museum? They could have just let themselves in through the front door."

"To make it look genuine of course," said Nina.

"Okay. That makes sense. But why are there three South Africans with him? Surely, they'd be Albanians if it was an inside job?"

"Maybe it's another way of hiding the real story."

"Maybe," I conceded. "But there's a flaw in your theory. As soon as they report the theft, the police will be crawling all over this place. They can't have a dormitory crammed with illegal immigrants in here then."

"No. They'd need to ship them out for a time," Nina agreed.

It was a puzzle, and we were slap bang in the middle of it. "There's another thing," I said to her. "What do they mean to do with us at the end of all this?"

"What do you mean?" asked Heloise, looking up.

"Well, I'm not sure they can afford to have us shooting our mouths off afterwards." Nina gave me a meaningful look which I interpreted as, 'don't scare Hel'. Fair enough. But I had already been scaring myself with the same question. I tried to figure it out. If Nick was carrying out an inside job, disguised to look like an outside job, then his Albanian masters wouldn't want any loose ends blabbing about underground dormitories and people trafficking. Not unless they had decided to abandon the tunnels and trade them in for a single enormous pay day. I realised I was clutching at straws in the hope of survival. No, if the Albanians were behind this theft, then it was likely that five fresh bodies would need to be disposed of before morning.

But if Nick was double-crossing his Albanian masters, either for himself or the South Africans, then we might have a chance of surviving the night. It might even be useful for him to have the police distracted by an operation to round up the illegal refugees. And yet, he still wouldn't want us - or them - left alive to point the finger at him and his gang. Not unless he had alternative identities lined up and a sure-fire way of getting out of the country quickly.

Where would he try to go with the silver? Transporting and hiding the stuff was going to be far from easy unless you had the logistics support and covert operations of a foreign government behind you. On balance, I still favoured my theory that this was a secret operation by the South Africans – but how I cursed myself for sharing it with Nick and his gang earlier on. If this was the truth, and they knew I suspected it, would they let me, and the others, survive the night?

Richard and Joyce re-joined us as the Albanians began to gather in small groups. The volume of conversation in the dormitory had risen and I sensed lots of eyes scrutinising us. "It's terrible, quite terrible," Richard was saying.

"Just two sinks and two toilets for all of these people," said Joyce. "And they were in such a state."

"It made me feel sick," added Richard. "I don't mind telling you."

He was interrupted by the door being kicked open again and the appearance of a gun barrel. The room hushed immediately. "Agimor," called Nick from outside. The big man hurried to the door. "Bring them out." Agimor turned and beckoned the other 39 people to follow him. Our little group waited as they all filed past and joined the end of the queue.

Outside, in the main tunnel, some lights had been turned on. They were suspended from rusting girders that crossed the tunnel and electric cables looped from one to another along its length. The Albanians were marshalled into a long line that snaked from the rear of one of the twelve-wheeled lorries into the open door of another room on the other side of the tunnel, directly opposite the dormitory. "You lot, get into the middle of the line," Nick said to us. "Tell everyone to make a space Agimor, and then close them up."

The five of us moved over into a gap in the line created by their foreman and five men at the front of the queue were told to climb into the shipping container on the lorry's trailer. Two of Nick's three chums were spaced along the length of the line with their pistol and their shotgun. The third must have been in the room with the silver because Nick studied a slip of paper and called through to him. "Okay. We can take 27 tonnes maximum in each trailer. Count them out and stop when you get to 1,063 bars."

I remembered there were 60 tonnes of the salvage haul in total. So, that meant Nick and his gang were being forced to leave 6 tonnes behind if they used just the two lorries. The ingots began to be passed out of the room and along the line. Each one was quite a weight and there was silence save for the occasional grunt as the men in the lorries began to stack them up. Nick's plan was falling into place. There was no way his gang could have loaded the lorries without exhausting themselves – even with the help of Heloise and the rest of us. But this captive workforce would quickly do the work for him.

I was counting each ingot as I took it from Nina and passed it on to Richard. I had only got to 289 when I heard Richard call out in anguish. There was a loud clatter as an ingot dropped and hit the floor. Joyce had collapsed into a heap and Richard had hurried over to her. "It's alright love, it's alright," he said, bending down onto one knee to cradle her head. He looked up at Nick. "She's exhausted," he said plaintively. "She can't do any more of this."

Nick shook his head in annoyance. "Alright. Take her to that chair over there. The rest of you, keep moving." The silver bars started moving along the human chain again while Richard helped his wife to a chair at the side of the tunnel. Nick vanished into the cab of the lorry and then climbed out holding a plastic bottle of water which he took over to Joyce. That was an encouraging sign. Perhaps he didn't want any bodies on his conscience after all.

CHAPTER 15

The monotony of passing the silver bars along the line stretched into the early morning. My stomach was still hurting from Nick's attack on me, and I could now feel my arms and shoulders protesting too. We were approaching the thousandth bar when an ear-piercing siren suddenly began to wail throughout the tunnel. The line stopped dead as everyone looked around and at each other in puzzlement. My heart leapt. It had to be some kind of security alarm. I looked across at Nick and was relieved to see how worried he looked. The two guards were looking panicked too. I saw a few men break out of the line and one went sprinting back to the security of the dormitory.

The siren continued for about thirty seconds before stopping. It was immediately followed by a well-spoken man's voice which crackled, as though out of a tannoy. *"This is the Wartime Broadcasting Service,"* he announced. *"This country has been attacked with nuclear weapons. Communications have been severely disrupted, and the number of casualties and the extent of the damage are not yet known. We shall bring you further information as soon as possible. Meanwhile stay tuned to this wavelength, stay calm and stay in your own house."*

Nick and his gang-of-three were now huddled together in the centre of the tunnel, talking furiously to each other and looking up and all around them. *"Remember there is nothing to be gained by trying to get away,"* the voice continued. *"By leaving your homes you could be exposing yourself to greater danger. If you leave, you may find yourself without food, without water, without accommodation and without protection. Radioactive fall-out, which follows a nuclear explosion, is many times more dangerous if you are directly exposed to it in the open. Roofs and walls offer substantial protection. The safest place is indoors."*

Or underground, I thought to myself. I realised we were listening to the famous four-minute warning that had been prepared by the government during the Cold War. But who was broadcasting it? And how? I had seen the wreckage of the tunnel's tannoy system for myself.

"Make sure gas and other fuel supplies are turned off and that all fires are extinguished. If mains water is available, this can be used for firefighting. You should also refill all your containers for drinking water after the fires have been put out, because the mains water supply may not be available for very long."

"Where's this coming from?" asked Nina.

"Search me," I said, "but it's rattled Nick and his henchmen."

Most of the Albanians were standing still and trying to understand what the disembodied voice was saying. It looked like the ones with better English were trying to translate it to some of the others. Perhaps they really thought a nuclear bomb had been dropped outside. A few were still drifting away, back to their dormitory. The silver bars had been dumped on the floor along the route of the human chain. One man was holding his stomach with both hands as he hurried into the shared bedroom. I guessed that he was carrying an ingot under his shirt.

"Water must not be used for flushing lavatories: until you are told that lavatories may be used again, other toilet arrangements must be made. Use your water only for essential drinking and cooking purposes. Water means life. Don't waste it."

"They would have played this here during rehearsals for a nuclear attack," said Nina.

"Yes, but who's playing it now?" I asked.

"Make your food stocks last: ration your supply, because it may have to last for 14 days or more. If you have fresh food in the house, use this first to avoid wasting it: food in tins will keep. If you live in an area where a fall-out warning has been given, stay in your fall-out room until you are told it is safe to come out. When the immediate

danger has passed, the sirens will sound a steady note. The "all clear" message will also be given on this wavelength. If you leave the fall-out room to go to the lavatory or replenish water food or water supplies, do not remain outside the room for a minute longer than is necessary."

"Jesus. It's scary, isn't it?" said Nina.

I nodded. I was only half-listening now as I watched Nick grappling with how to restore order to the loading operation. I had my answer very quickly as he pointed his shotgun at the ceiling of the big tunnel and pulled the trigger. The explosion sounded enormous as it echoed around the underground chamber, and it temporarily masked the soundtrack of the nuclear warning. Immediately afterwards, he shouted as loudly as he could, "Back in line everyone. Get back in line now."

But the voice continued relentlessly with its calm and well-modulated pronunciation. *"Do not, in any circumstances, go outside the house. Radioactive fall-out can kill. You cannot see it or feel it, but it is there. If you go outside, you will bring danger to your family and you may die. Stay in your fall-out room until you are told it is safe to come out or you hear the "all clear" on the sirens."*

Nick and his gang were now marshalling people back to the line with their guns. The little man, or Bunce as I called him, had been sent into the dormitory and the Albanians were reluctantly emerging through the door. But still the voice went on: *"Here are the main points again: Stay in your own homes, and if you live in an area where a fall-out warning has been given, stay in your fall-out room, until you are told it is safe to come out. The message that the immediate danger has passed will be given by the sirens and repeated on this wavelength. Make sure that the gas and all fuel supplies are turned off and that all fires are extinguished."*

Nina, Heloise and I were waved back into our previous positions and we all bent down to pick up the silver bars from the floor. The voice carried on.

"Water must be rationed and used only for essential drinking and cooking purposes. It must not be used for flushing lavatories. Ration your food supply – it may have to last for 14 days or more."

"Alright!" shouted Nick. "Start moving." The line began to work again.

"*We shall be on the air every hour, on the hour. Stay tuned to this wavelength, but switch off your radios now to save your batteries. That is the end of this broadcast.*"

The sudden silence prompted another burst of excited chatter along the line which Nick ended by firing another shotgun cartridge into the ceiling. "Be quiet," he shouted. "Hesht. Hesht."

His slaves army got the message and the heavy silver bars kept coming once again. I saw Nick in conference with Boggis out of the corner of my eye. The large man set off quickly down the route we had come. I imagined he had been despatched to check there was no-one in the museum tunnels who had somehow triggered the recording of the four-minute warning. Such a message would have been intended to be broadcast from the little BBC studio that I had seen on my tour. But the equipment in the studio had looked totally broken and redundant to me. I checked my watch. It was nearly 3 a.m. now. The interruption of the tannoy had probably wasted twenty minutes or so. Nick had reacted quickly and restored order before the recording had finished. Nevertheless, it had cost him time and I wondered what kind of schedule he was working to. Presumably, he would want to drive the lorries out under cover of darkness. Sunrise would be at around 7 a.m. I calculated that he would manage it quite easily at the current rate of loading – unless there were more interruptions. And there were.

CHAPTER 16

Finally, no more ingots came down the line and I passed the last one to Nina roughly ten minutes after the work had restarted. Agimor came along telling everyone to sit down where they were and to rest for ten minutes. I laid down, flat on my back and stared up at the tunnel roof which was painted white and scarred and scratched with the signs of its construction. Nina had done the same and her head was close to mine.

"Well, Jack Johnson. You certainly know how to show a girl a good time."

I rubbed my eyes. I felt thoroughly fatigued. "It's good to know we're paying four hundred pounds for the privilege of working underground in a chain gang."

"And doesn't it make your heart sing to know we're doing it to make the odious Nick as rich as Croesus?"

"May he rot in hell," added Heloise who had overheard our exchange. She was rummaging about in her shoulder bag on the floor, but emerged empty handed.

The man in question strolled past at that moment. I could tell he was anxious to begin loading the second lorry, but Agimor had been insistent that everyone should have a rest, and he needed to keep his gang-leader on side. There was still no sign of Boggis's return and I didn't envy him wandering around the museum's tunnels on his own by torchlight. No doubt, he'd been ordered to check out the BBC studio and the rusting remains of the tannoy system. What were the chances of him getting completely lost, I wondered? And could the remaining three men, armed with a shotgun, a pistol and a knife, really maintain control over us and 40 Albanians? It was precisely at that moment that the mist appeared.

We were alerted to it by a young man who had stood up and was pointing towards the end of the tunnel furthest away from the entrance. I didn't understand his words but there was no mistaking the alarm in them. I sat up to look and then I stood up to check that I wasn't imagining it. Nina stood up with me and almost everyone else was now doing the same.

A wall of fog was swirling across the full width and height of the tunnel. Moreover, it appeared to be slowly moving towards us. It took a few seconds to sink in before pandemonium broke out. Agimor was pointing at it and shouting "Fire! Fire". His countrymen and women were running in all directions and shouting too. I could understand their panic. The idea of being trapped underground while a fire spread throughout the complex was too terrible to contemplate. If the flames didn't kill us, the smoke undoubtedly would.

I rushed over to Nick who was staring open-mouthed at the approaching wall. "You've got to let these people out," I shouted at him. I put a hand on his arm which seemed to jolt him to his senses. "For God's sake," I shouted, "help them get away from the fire."

"Shut up," he snarled at me. Then he did something I wasn't expecting at all. He broke his shotgun and extracted the two green cartridges. Then he thrust the gun into my hands and snapped, "Hold this." I did as I was told and watched as he sprinted across to the dormitory, entered it, and reappeared moments later holding a large red fire extinguisher.

He extended an arm and pointed it at me as he ran towards the fog or smoke or whatever it was. "Watch him," he shouted across to Bean who was standing still and staring helplessly at the bedlam with his pistol dangling down by his side.

And then Nick disappeared. He simply ran into the centre of the swirling whiteness and vanished. His greed had made him foolhardy. He had obviously decided to risk everything by trying to find the source of the fire, if that's what it was. But surely, I thought, he'd be rapidly overcome by the thickness of the smoke.

Still, it came on and on, moving relentlessly towards us at a slow walking pace. Everyone except Nick had continued to back away from it and several had fled all the way to the enormous doors at the far end of the tunnel. I could hear them trying to bang on them, but they were making little impact and little noise. The main entrance would be made of thick metal and built to withstand a nuclear blast.

I quickly moved over to Richard and Joyce who were still sitting at the side of the tunnel close to a lorry. Nina and Heloise had followed me. Richard started with surprise when he saw I was carrying a shotgun. Joyce did not look at all well. She was shivering with her arms wrapped around herself and her eyes were blank. I don't think she had registered what was happening at all.

"Let's stick together," I said.

"Let's try to find the way back into the museum," said Nina. "It might buy us some time if it is a fire."

"Good idea," I said.

But Heloise stalled us before we could get moving. "Look," she said urgently. She was pointing back down the tunnel where Nick had re-emerged from the swirling wall. We watched as he hurled the fire extinguisher away from him in disgust. It bounced and clattered and finally spun to a stop against the side of the tunnel. Then he marched straight up to our little group and snatched the gun back off me.

"You've got to let these people out," I told him again. "If the flames don't get them, the smoke will. It'll be mass murder."

"It's not smoke," he spat. "It's steam - or some kind of mist. It's just water vapour. That's all. There must be a leaky pipe somewhere." He wiped his hair with a hand and I realised it was wet. The shoulders of his coat were also dark with damp. He broke the gun to reload it with the cartridges from his pocket. "Agimor!" he shouted, looking all around. "Where the hell are you?"

I looked back at the wall again. It no longer seemed to be

advancing on us. "Come on, let's have a look," I said to Nina.

She joined me to walk towards the cloud, took hold of my hand and stepped into it with me. Surprisingly, there was still some visibility as the mist swirled all around us. It certainly didn't smell like smoke from a fire. Nick was right, it felt damp and moist on our skin. The visibility even seemed to be improving as we stood there. Yes, it seemed as though it was dissipating quite fast now. I looked up. I could see the roof of the tunnel emerging above me. I had no idea where the bank of mist had come from, or where it was going. But in the end, it trailed away as quickly as it came and there was barely a wisp of it left after a couple of minutes.

"Well, that was baffling," Nina said.

"That must have put him behind schedule," I replied. I checked my watch. "Quarter to four. I reckon he'll try to get away before it's light. He'll need to travel in the dark. He's running out of time."

It was almost as though Nick had heard me. He was running around like a man possessed, or like a sheepdog frantically trying to round up a flock that had scattered in all directions. In the end, he decided the best tactic was for him, Agimor and the two others to line up across the entrance door and then sweep back up the tunnel, urging the Albanians back towards the lorries. It was a sullen and mutinous crowd which was finally corralled into a group outside the rear of the second lorry. But Nick was nothing if not resourceful. He jumped up into the second shipping container and pulled Agimor up alongside him. "Hesht. Hesht," he called out and the muttering slowly fizzled out.

"Agimor, tell them this. When I leave in an hour or so, there will be 6 tonnes of silver left behind in the tunnel." Agimor translated this in a deep voice. "We can't take it with us. It would be too heavy for the lorries." Once again, Agimor turned Nick's words into Albanian. The crowd was now quiet. They were all looking at each other and back up at the two men above them. Nick had their full attention. "That silver is worth £3.2 million. That is more than 430 million lek in your own currency." An excited chatter greeted Agimor's translation of these numbers. "It's yours to keep," said Nick dramatically and holding out his hands. "You will be rich beyond your wildest dreams if you all work hard now and help me load the second trailer." Agimor's excitement was palpable as he told them this. There was a cheer and a round of clapping. Many of them shook hands or hugged each other. "It will pay for your new life in a new country!" declaimed Nick with a final flourish. His words were met with a ragged cheer.

The second line formed with alacrity and the speed of delivery of the second batch of silver was almost twice as fast as the first. I assumed it would be identical in size to the first - 1,063 bars. The activity was relentless. I stood sideways and swivelled my waist to take an ingot from Nina before swivelling again, with the weight in two hands, to pass it to Heloise. She too was standing sideways with her feet spread either side of her shoulder bag. There was no opportunity to check my watch, but I knew the pace had picked up in spite of everyone's tiredness. Nick had found a way to motivate the Albanians with his promise of a share of the loot.

However, as I was approaching the thousandth ingot in my head, the tunnel was filled with sound again. This time, I recognised the sonorous bongs of Big Ben striking the hour. The line paused again, but there was no widespread agitation as there had been when the nuclear siren alert had sounded. A man's serious voice crackled into life.

"This is the BBC's home and service programme. Here is the news and this is Bruce Belfrage reading it. There is an admiralty communique giving the full story of recent naval successes in the Mediterranean."

I immediately recognised this as the words of a BBC radio news broadcast from the Second World War. But how was it being broadcast now, in this tunnel, nearly eighty years after the war had ended? The human chain remained in place this time, although it paused work as Bruce Belfrage continued with his bulletin.

"Besides the latest details of RAF successes against Berlin and other

vital objectives, there is more news of the good results of our air raids in Africa. More daylight air attacks by enemy fighters have been broken up. There is comment both from Moscow and from London on the news from Rumania."

But the Albanians were now inured to the received pronunciation emerging out of the ether. There had been no siren to scatter them this time, and most of them wouldn't have been able to understand what the words meant. Nick strode to the point in the line where an Albanian woman was empty handed and urged her to take the ingot that was waiting for her. It prompted the whole line to swing back into action. Bruce seemed to get the message.

"Tonight's talk, after this bulletin, will be by Lord Lloyd, the colonial secretary," he said rather lamely. But there was no sign of the rest of the bulletin. He just suddenly finished speaking and the silver bars maintained their continuous passage along the line.

The bulky frame of Boggis had reappeared in the main tunnel while the bulletin was being transmitted. But the shrug of his shoulders and his outspread hands told Nick that he had been unable to find anyone next door or the source of the strange broadcasts. Nick, who was eagerly eyeing the ingots disappearing into the lorry, waved at him with indifference. His plan was working out.

CHAPTER 17

It was quarter to five in the morning as the last silver bar found its way through the hands of 43 people and up into the second lorry's trailer. Richard and Joyce had been excused from returning to work. The couple had remained slumped on the floor throughout the night. They were a picture of misery whenever I glanced across at them and they had both been asleep at one point.

The two metal doors of the container were swung shut with a loud clang and padlocked. Agimor called out something and was rewarded with a big cheer. He strode towards the vault which had stored the silver and several of the Albanians crowded in after him to see what the remaining haul of three million and two hundred thousand pounds looked like. It would be interesting to see how cheerful and friendly they all remained once the difficult work of splitting their cut and cashing it in was underway.

Nick checked his watch and summoned his gang for a quick conference. I moved across to re-join Richard and Joyce with Nina and Heloise.

"What happens now?" asked Heloise.

"They open the front door and drive off into a rich new dawn I suppose," I said.

"What happens to us, she means," said Nina.

"I honestly don't know. I think it all depends on who they're working for," I said, "and how confident they are about their escape route."

"We just want to go home," wailed Richard. His wife was rigid and silent. She looked catatonic.

"Alright, follow me," said Nick. He had walked over to us with Bunce who was still gripping his pistol. I saw the other two were bent over the rear of one of the lorries. It looked like they were changing the number plates. We fell into line behind Nick and retraced our route to the stepladder which we were made to climb in turn. We were ushered back along the duct and down into the museum again. Joyce struggled even more with the physical exertion this time. She ended up being cajoled and manhandled through the obstacle course by Richard and me. She was still whimpering as we gathered at the foot of the second stepladder.

"Look," I said angrily and stepping up close to Nick. "She's in no condition for any more of this. What are you planning to do with us?"

He smiled nastily at me. "Watch your mouth. Unless you want another stomach-ache. Well. Do you?" His shotgun had been strapped to his back again for the return journey through the duct, but he was fingering it threateningly. Nina held my arm and pulled me back slightly. "Help him with her," he ordered brusquely. I linked my arm under Joyce and Richard did the same. We both half carried and half dragged her back through the museum's rooms and passageways until we reached the BBC studio.

"In there." We all filed in and watched as he placed a full bottle of water and a single torch upright on the studio's broadcasting desk. "Well, it's time for me to love you and leave you. The head of tours will come looking for you when he realises that I haven't returned his keys. You'll probably be out by lunchtime." He walked over to Heloise. "Bye Hel. It's been nice knowing you. But you need to stop all this fortune telling nonsense. It's all a lot of crap isn't it? Still, at least you've got a bit of cash out of it – unless you give them all a refund of course." Heloise's startling blue eyes stared up at him in the darkness, full of loathing.

He laughed to himself and then checked his watch. "Right," he turned to the tall thin man in the doorway. "We've got an hour to go. Bang on schedule," he grinned. "I do love it when a plan works out."

He turned on his heel, closed the door firmly and we heard him clicking a padlock shut. The room was solely lit by the torch on the table which was pointing up towards a broken suspended ceiling. It must have been installed to improve sound quality in the little studio. I picked up the torch and used it to do a quick inspection of our prison cell. The thick metal door seemed too solid to break down. Perhaps we could break the large glass window which looked out into the production area? But it looked to be double or even triple-glazed for acoustic reasons and there was no obvious tool to use.

I shone the torch on Joyce who was slumped against a wall and being cuddled by Richard. "She's in a bad way," said Heloise as she slipped the strap of her bag over her head and dumped it on the floor before sitting down next to the older woman. "I think she's having some kind of attack."

"She needs a doctor," moaned Richard.

I took the top off the bottle of water and gave it to Heloise who trickled some into Joyce's mouth. Then we all took a mouthful in turn, and I returned the bottle to the table. Nina sidled over to sit beside me.

"We need to get out of here well before lunchtime," she said. "Joyce needs medical attention."

"I know," I said. "But our phones won't work, and I can't see a way to get out of here." Nick seemed to suggest they would be leaving in another hour. That meant he was waiting for first light rather than going out under the cover of darkness. I didn't understand his reasoning, unless he thought the lorries would be more inconspicuous if they blended into the early morning rush-hour.

I was puzzling this out when there was a thud from the centre of the room. I turned the torchlight onto the table. The plastic water bottle had gone. I shone the torch onto the floor and there it was, lying on its side with the remaining water escaping to form a puddle.

"Quick, save it," said Nina.

Heloise was the closest and she scuttled over to pick up the bottle. Then, in a strange voice, she added, "Jack, over here. Quick, bring the torch."

Nina and I moved over to join her. I shone the torch onto the little pool of water. Then Heloise suddenly leaned forward onto her knees and dipped her forefinger into the puddle.

"Bloody hell," said Nina.

Below us, in the space between us, the young woman's finger was using the puddle to write something in the dust and dirt of the floor. And as the watery letters slowly emerged, one after another, I recognised the joined-up handwriting that had been created earlier by the planchette. An ice-cold sensation prickled the back of my neck. "It's Gilbert!" I whispered.

The writing continued and then stopped. We all bent closer to try to make it out.

"The Devil's Den!" said Nina.

Sure enough, we could now make out the three words that Heloise had traced in the water.

TheDevil'sDen

"What about it?" asked Nina in a puzzled voice.

Heloise dipped her finger in the water again and began to trace a single line away into the darkness and outside the torch's pool of light. I adjusted the torch to follow her. She crawled for a couple of metres, continuing to draw the line until she reached a large old cupboard made of metal. Then she ended the line with an arrowhead that pointed directly at the cupboard. There had been barely any water left by the time it reached this point and we watched as the direction arrow began to evaporate in front of us. Nina shone the torch back towards the handwriting and it too was distinctly smaller and less distinct as the water seeped into the sandstone floor.

"He's trying to help us," said Heloise in amazement. "Gilbert's trying to help us."

I shook my head. This was crazy. I had assumed that Hel had been directing the planchette during the séance. Was she doing something similar now?

"He's showing us a way to the Devil's Den," said Nina excitedly. She took the torch from me and swung open one of the large doors on the metal cupboard. The shelves were empty except for a few plastic reels that would have held magnetic recording tape. She opened the other door. It was empty. She reached through a gap between the shelves and banged on the back of the cupboard. It was solid metal.

"Let's try to shift it," I said. The three of us tried to prise the tips of our fingers behind the rear of the cupboard, but it was tight up against the wall.

"Can we tip it forward?" asked Nina.

"It's worth a go," I said. "Give Richard the torch and let's bring the table over." We scraped the table over to one side of the cupboard and Nina and I climbed up on top of it. "Stand clear." We both looped our hands under the metal rim and pulled with as much force as we could muster. I could feel it starting to pivot forward. "Give it a shove from behind," I said to Heloise. The cupboard fell forward seconds later with an enormous metallic crash.

Richard shone the torch onto the wall behind. A piece of hardboard was fixed to the stone. It was the width of the cupboard and about a metre high. I tried to dig my fingernails into its top and pull it backwards. Then we all tried but it refused to budge. Yet it must have been there for decades and surely it had become weak and flimsy with age?

"Stand back," I said, and took a running kick at the centre of the board. My foot disappeared through it and Nina grabbed me as I threatened to topple over. I yanked it out and stamped down on the hole with my heel. A piece broke off. The others now bent down and began desperately ripping out pieces to make the hole bigger. "Hang on a minute," I said. I retrieved the torch from

Richard and shone it through the hole. There, in front of me, was a red sandstone tunnel stretching away as far as the torch beam would go. Nina had a look followed by Heloise.

"It must go all the way to The Devil's Den," I said in wonderment. "It must have been created as some kind of escape tunnel for the miners."

"Thank you, Gilbert," whispered Heloise. I looked hard at her and tried to make sense of what had just happened. How could she have known about a hidden tunnel behind the metal cupboard? And yet, if she hadn't, how had we come to be told about it?

I looked back at Joyce's stricken white face. "Will you stay with them if Nina and I try to go for help?" I asked. "I don't think she's up to crawling down there."

Heloise bit her lip but nodded briefly. "Don't be long."

"Good luck," added Richard. "Take the torch. You'll need it more than us."

I nodded. He was right but I didn't relish leaving them in the pitch blackness.

"Come on," said Nina. "We need to move fast."

CHAPTER 18

I'd rather not dwell on the thirty minutes that followed this decision. It was awkward trying to crawl on our hands and knees and I was also trying to hold the torch. My wrists were in agony after ten minutes and I would occasionally scrape my head against the roof of the little tunnel. The air became increasingly stale, and our breathing was more and more laboured, both through exhaustion and a lack of fresh oxygen.

I tried to picture my Ordnance Survey map as I crawled forward and calculated that if the tunnel followed the most direct route, it would be about a mile between our starting point in the BBC studio and our destination, The Devil's Den. But there was a huge difference between a twenty-minute stroll along the towpath and the torture of doing it on all fours in a confined space.

At one point I stopped and panted to Nina, "D'you want to sit and have a rest?" In truth, it was more for my benefit than hers.

"We can't," she panted back. "We've got to get help for Joyce. And we've got to stop Nick. Keep going Jack. I'll take the lead if you want."

I examined my watch. It was 5.35 a.m. "Okay, you take a turn with the torch." She wriggled past me and set off immediately. I have to confess Nina set a faster pace than me and a gap opened up between us. This meant it was darker in my immediate vicinity. The light of the torch bounced around ahead of me in Nina's hand. My back and shoulders were on fire and the palms of my hands were raw. I reckoned my knees had been ruined for life.

My mind was also in a bad place. I took little comfort as I thought of the worst things that could happen. What if it proved impossible to access the little boathouse at the end of the tunnel? It could easily be blocked, either by natural causes such as a cave-in, or deliberately by British Waterways when they sealed the entrance. I genuinely doubted my ability to simply turn around and crawl all the way back to the others. But there would be no alternative.

"We're here, I think," called Nina from up ahead. I checked my watch again. We had been crawling for the best part of 40 minutes.

I shuffled forward as fast as I could, praying that I wouldn't be met by the sight of an impregnable pile of stone and boulders. It was hard to see much beyond Nina's body, but I moved alongside her as closely as the space permitted. We seemed to be confronted by another sheet of hardboard. Nina was pushing against it with both palms, trying it for strength.

"I think it'll give," she said. "But it's hard to get much leverage against it."

There was no chance of giving it a running kick this time. But there was no way on earth that I was going to be forced to make a return trip. "Let's try to lie on our backs, next to each other, and kick it with our feet," I suggested.

We manoeuvred ourselves into position with considerable difficulty. Nina was still holding the torch in one hand, and it was shining upwards onto the tunnel roof close above us. "Move closer towards it," I said. We needed to exert maximum force on it. I planted both feet halfway up the board and Nina did likewise. "Okay. On 3. 1 -2 -3 Push!"

I felt the board sag outwards a little but otherwise, nothing else happened. "Okay," I said with gritted teeth. "Let's try to kick it together, rather than just pushing. Pull your knees back." We both withdrew our feet from the board and held them suspended in the air. "Ready? Big kick on 3 again. 1 - 2 - 3."

Nothing. "Again," I said. "But harder and then keep kicking. 1 - 2 - 3." This time we banged and banged and banged away at the board, hitting it as hard as we possibly could with both feet, bending our knees and using our thighs to thrust forward. I could feel a slight give, but I was unsure whether it was the board loosening its fixtures on the other side or simply sagging in the middle. We both gave up at the same time and lay there with our chests heaving.

"Again," said Nina. I groaned. "Come on," she urged. We mounted another assault on the wretched board until Nina said, "Stop." I shuffled backwards slightly so I could drop my aching legs flat onto the floor. "We aren't hitting it at the same time," she said, breathing heavily. "We need to be more co-ordinated. Take a breather for a moment. I'll turn the torch off to save the battery."

We lay there, side by side in the total darkness. I closed my eyes. I was so tired. It would be so easy to fall into a deep sleep now. I may even have given in to this thought because I started when Nina broke the all-enveloping silence. "Ok Jack? Ready for one almighty kick?" The torch came back on and blinded me for a moment.

I grunted. I needed to save my breath. We shuffled forward on our backs into the strike position again. "On 3 again then, Jack. Ready? 1 - 2 -3." This time our feet struck the board at exactly the same time. Nina called out again, "And 3." We hit it together for a second time. "Again. And 3." It was the fifth co-ordinated kick which ended with both our feet smashing through the board and bursting through to the other side. Nina was the first to scramble onto her knees and begin tearing at the ragged hole with both hands, pulling off pieces of board and throwing them behind us. I joined her until we had a gap large enough to squeeze through.

I picked up the torch, put one arm and head through the hole and shone it around on the other side. A large square space had been built into the cliff with a ledge immediately in front of us and I could see water beyond it. This had to be the boathouse. I pulled myself back through the hole in the board. "We're there," I said to Nina.

She took the torch from me, wriggled through the gap and then helped to pull me through after her. We stood up on the ledge and immediately felt a flurry of activity going on above us. Bats. Nina shone the torch upwards where clusters of black shapes hung from the roof. Some had already detached themselves and were flitting around, disturbing the air near our heads as they swirled and circled. I felt a bat's wing smack against the back of my head.

Nina shone the torch across the water at the oak door. There wouldn't be any way of kicking a hole in that, and I knew it was solidly fastened by a padlock on the outside. But I also knew the cave had been excavated to allow the Foley family's leisure craft to go in and out. That must mean the canal water flowed under the door to allow room for the hulls of their boats. And if boats could go in and out under the door, then we could too, as long as we were prepared to get wet. I explained my theory briefly to Nina.

She looked at the dark expanse of cold water and once again above her head at the roof of the cave and the swirling black shapes. "Will this night never end?" she sighed. "But wait. Why don't we just use our phones now?"

I fished mine out of my back pocket and brought it to life. "Still no signal," I said. That wasn't surprising. There had barely been a signal on Jumping Jack Flash, and we were still in an underground space surrounded by solid sandstone.

Nina checked her phone and came up with the same result. "But if we swim for it, our phones will be no use anyway."

I agreed. "We might as well leave them here rather than wreck them. We can fetch them later."

"So, what's the plan?" she asked.

"I'll swim under the door and across the canal. I can fetch the bike off the boat and cycle down to the lock cottage. I'll see if I can phone the police from there. You can wait here."

"Fat chance, matey," she said. "I'm coming with you." I shrugged and kneeled down to begin unlacing my walking boots. Nina sat down to do the same. I looked across at the little oak door. "What are you thinking?" asked Nina.

"I'm weighing up what else to take off. We'll need to swim fast and straight and not have anything snag underwater. But it's going to be freezing."

"Well, your clothes aren't going to keep you warm in the water, are they? And they won't be much use when we get out either. We can get into some dry things on the boat. It won't take long to get dressed again." She was right and so we both stripped off to our underwear and stood there shivering on the ledge. I checked my watch. It was 5.50 a.m.

"Come on, let's do this," she said. She sat down with her legs dangling into the water. Then she took her bearing on the door and slipped forward. She gasped at the cold immersion and then kicked off to swim breaststroke to the entrance. When she reached it, she didn't look back but simply took a big breath, sank underwater and didn't reappear. I took this as a good sign. She must have just ducked under the bottom edge of the door and resurfaced on the other side. I sat down on the ledge in my boxer shorts. I held my boat key in one fist. Its keyring was a little inflatable ball of cork. Then I too slipped into the water. Bloody hell! It was freezing.

An early morning jogger or dog walker would have been astonished to see a mostly naked couple leveraging themselves out of the Staffs & Worcs Canal that morning. Fortunately, or unfortunately, the towpath opposite The Devil's Den was completely deserted. We immediately began jogging the short distance around the corner to the boat where Eddie barked protectively and then danced ecstatically around us as we quickly climbed into several layers of dry clothes. I locked him back on board, much to his disgust, and we pedalled fast to Stewponey Lock where I banged on the door of a white cottage on the old wharf.

The door was eventually opened by a suspicious old chap in a paisley dressing gown and slippers. It took at least five minutes before he conceded we could use his landline to ring the police, and only if we stayed outside on the doorstep. I checked my watch while he went to fetch the handset. It was now 6.10 a.m. I pictured Richard, Joyce and Heloise still sitting there in the dark, wondering if we had got through and anxious to be released. And I imagined Nick and his gang, congratulating themselves and preparing to move the lorries to wherever they had planned. I wondered if they had locked the Albanians back in the dormitory or left them free to escape the tunnels and roam across the country with their silver ingots.

These thoughts gave some urgency to my demands for a rapid police presence at The Millionaire Tunnels. Eventually, the emergency operator patched me through to a duty police inspector who asked a short sequence of intelligent questions. At the end he said, "Okay, I need to make some calls Mr Johnson. But if this is some kind of wind-up, I warn you, we will hunt you to the ends of the earth and throw the book at you."

I understood his doubts. My tale of an ongoing heist for shipwrecked silver bars worth £32 million and an underground hideaway for 40 illegal immigrants sounded incredible to my ears too. And I hadn't even begun to describe the strange goings-on we had witnessed in the tunnels. If I had, he would have undoubtedly put me down as a lunatic or an early-morning drunk.

Nina and I thanked the old man and cycled as fast as we could to the main entrance of the warehouse. This looked much more secure than the entrance to the museum part of the complex. The parking area immediately outside the large doors was flooded in light and a small guard hut was well-lit to the side of some strong-looking perimeter gates. As we approached, I could see two figures in the hut.

"Keep cycling," I said to Nina, and we pedalled on past the entrance before stopping to lean our bikes against the fence. "We don't know if the outside guards have been bought off by Nick. Let's just wait for the police," I said. "We don't want them warning him."

It was another 15 minutes before the first marked police car arrived. Fortunately, it came from our direction and I was able to flag it down before it reached the entrance. I introduced myself to two young constables in uniform. "Please tell me they've sent more than you," I said.

The driver looked annoyed, but his mate just laughed. "No, the cavalry is on its way." Sure enough, four more police cars arrived shortly afterwards including one with a senior ranking officer inside. He strode over to me and Nina, checked we were the people who had raised the alarm and told us to stay where we were. "You're certain they're armed?" he asked.

"Yes. Two shotguns and a pistol." He nodded grimly. His arrival was followed by two large blue vans and another a few minutes later. The senior offer held a short discussion with four officers at the side of the road. Two of them were wearing bullet proof vests and carrying helmets and guns.

Then we watched as the vans approached the entrance gate. The rear doors of the first one opened and a firearms unit, all dressed in black and wearing protective clothing, spilled out. They were pointing their guns at the guard hut and shouting. The main gates were quickly swung open. The parking, unloading and loading area in front of the warehouse was soon full of police cars and the three vans were strung out in a line immediately in front of the warehouse door. The second and third vans had been carrying more firearms officers who took up their positions. Two officers were now standing in the guard hut with the two security guards we had seen earlier.

I checked my watch. It said 6.55 a.m. The sky was lightening quickly but there was no civilian traffic going past on the road. I assumed the police had been busy putting up road blocks. The senior officer came back to stand close to me. "You think they're going to leave at seven?" he asked again.

I nodded, praying that there hadn't been a change of plan and that Nick had already gone. "We're going in as soon as the big door starts to open," he said. "I don't want it getting high enough to let the lorries out. If they're as big as you say, they could easily crash their way through our cordon and the gates." I nodded. It was a brave call because it meant his officers might be rushing in to face gunfire from Nick and his gang. "It's happening," he said urgently.

Sure enough, there was a rumble of machinery in the quiet morning air. A gap was beginning to emerge at the bottom of the warehouse door as it began to roll upwards into the main tunnel's roofspace. Almost immediately, armed black figures moved forward in a line and began rolling or bending themselves under the rising door. It had reached the height of a car roof before it stopped. "Good," muttered the policeman. "What the hell!"

As we were watching, men began crouching under the door and running in all directions. It was the Albanians. They were looking left and right, dodging and ducking as they sprinted through the parked police cars in a desperate effort to escape. I noticed that many of them seemed to be carrying heavy weights – the silver ingots. However, there was only one way out of the compound, and it was heavily guarded by a phalanx of armed and unarmed officers. Some of the Albanians were ordered to kneel at gunpoint and obeyed instantly. A few of the others were wrestled to the ground and handcuffed.

What was happening inside? I could see the headlights of the first lorry were on, but it didn't seem to have moved any closer to the entrance. A voice crackled in the senior policeman's earpiece. "Roger, well done," he replied. "We've got them. No casualties," he smiled. He strode off towards the gate's entrance and we fell into step with him. He didn't seem to mind. All the discomfort of the crawl through the tunnel and our icy underwater swim didn't count for anything compared to the heart-warming scene that now greeted us. Nick and the three South Africans were being escorted out of the tunnel with their hands secured behind their backs and two armed officers flanking each of them. "Is that all of them?"

"It is," I confirmed, smiling broadly at Nick. "Good morning, Nick."

The four men gaped at us. "What the …?" said the tall thin man. "You! How did you get out?"

"You bastard," spat Nick. He tried to struggle free. I heard Nina give a little giggle next to me.

"An old friend showed us the way," I said as he was ushered past us.

All four men were loaded into the back of two police cars. One of the armed officers had been following the group. He waited until the car doors were slammed shut and then turned back to approach us. "Well done, sergeant," said the senior police officer.

"They were all in the lorry cabs when we went in," the other replied. "But they came quietly when they saw our numbers. Good job they didn't get those rigs rolling." He looked around the parking area where the Albanians were all being rounded up and cuffed. "There's a few more inside. My lads will bring them all out."

His words gave me a jolt. There were three other people who needed to be brought out as quickly as possible. "Our friends are still in the museum," I said to the officer in charge. "We need to get them, urgently."

"Under control," he nodded. "We sent someone to fetch the keyholder." He walked off a few paces, muttered into his radio and listened to a reply before turning back to us. "Why don't you go round now with my sergeant here? I need to wait for a coach for this lot and the scene-of-crime team."

It took a few minutes to walk to the entrance of the museum tunnels and a police car was already in the car park alongside an ambulance with its rear doors open. The main door to the tunnels was also open and we could see it was lit inside. We walked past the decontamination room on the right and into the entrance foyer just as two paramedics appeared pushing Joyce in a wheelchair, with Richard anxiously following behind. "You did it!" he exclaimed, pumping my hand and hugging Nina. "Thank you. Thank you so much."

"How's Joyce?" I asked.

"They think she'll be alright. But it looks like some kind of heart attack again. I must stay with her," he said, bustling off. "Thank you."

I looked up to see Nina giving Heloise a tight hug and after she finished, I did the same. Two more uniformed police officers walked past accompanied by a middle-aged man in overalls and a fluorescent yellow tabard. He was holding a big bunch of keys. He looked like a very worried man.

"We'd better get back to the boss," said the sergeant. "I'm afraid you've got a long morning ahead, giving statements and so on. I bet you're dying for a hot mug of tea."

We all began to make our way back to the entrance when Heloise suddenly stopped. There was a stone memorial plaque on the wall dedicated to the memory of those who died during the construction of The Millionaire Tunnels. The fourth name on the list was Gilbert. Gilbert Shaw.

Nina, Hel and I stared at it while the sergeant continued to chatter on. "I just don't understand how you managed to find a way out and tip us off," he was saying.

Heloise adjusted the strap of her shoulder bag, reached across and touched Gilbert's name on the plaque. She smiled and said softly, "We had inside help." Then she lifted her head to look up and around the tunnel. Her eyes were glittering with emotion. "But he's saved at least one life today. I hope he's at peace now."

"Amen to that," said Nina who linked arms with her new friend and led the way out into the fresh cold morning air.

CHAPTER 19

I persuaded our police driver to let us call in at Jumping Jack Flash so that I could feed Eddie and give him a brief walk. Then, as the sergeant had promised, we spent a few hours being interviewed at the main police station in Wolverhampton and signing our written statements. We were totally exhausted by the time we were delivered back to Jumping Jack Flash where we slept deeply throughout the afternoon.

I was blearily making tea when there was a knock on the door of the boat. I was stiff all over from my part in the human chain and the crawl through the tunnel and so I hobbled painfully to the stern. It was the senior police officer who had presided over the arrests. He had eventually introduced himself as Chief Inspector Brian Gibson. He had Heloise with him and his sergeant.

"Hello there," he said, shaking my hand. "Please forgive the intrusion. I thought you might both be rested by now and appreciate a bit of an update. Ah excellent, is that a fresh pot of tea? Enough to go round is there?" I had quickly decided, earlier in the day, that I liked the Chief Inspector. He had been very quick to respond to the urgent briefing from the duty inspector and his operation had been briskly and efficiently organised and carried out.

He settled into an armchair and encouraged Eddie to jump up onto his lap where he ruffled the fur on his chest. "All this is off the record, of course. So, nothing in the papers, please." He gave me a meaningful look. He now knew something of our background. "We don't want to go screwing up a trial, do we?"

"Understood," I said. "You have my word - until the court case is over."

"Good. Well, you told us there were 40 Albanians down there in total and we've rounded them all up. They've all gone off to a Home Office detention centre now. Of course, they're staying completely silent over how they got into the country and whoever organised it. We're trying to dig into the ownership of the tunnels to see if that sheds any light. They probably came in the backs of lorries and, no doubt, there were a few bribes or threats to look the other way at the ports. It was obviously a big operation. Safer than a rubber dinghy across the English Channel, eh? Especially at this time of year. But a lot more expensive. I'm told they pay up to £20,000 each to come in by lorry. Well, they'll be deported back home as soon as possible. And I don't imagine they'll be getting a refund, the poor beggars. I don't think they could have been down in the tunnels for long. It was probably just somewhere they could all be delivered out of sight and then slowly released as inconspicuously as possible." He took a noisy slurp of his tea.

"As for the silver," he smiled. "According to the figures you gave us, all but one bar was recovered and it's all safely under lock and key by now, waiting for its rightful owner. The court decided it was legal salvage a few days ago and threw out the claim by the South African government. So, the owner had to move it out of the customs warehouse at Southampton in a hurry. It seems he didn't choose his new storage facility very carefully. He probably thought it was safe as houses in a secret location underground. I imagine he'll be very grateful to you when he hears the whole story. By the way," he added, looking around at all three of us. "I don't suppose any of you know anything about the missing ingot?"

The others all shook their heads. "I think I saw at least one being taken into the dormitory after the siren sounded on the tannoy system," I said.

He nodded. "Well, if it's still down there, we'll find it."

"But what about Nick and the South Africans?" I asked. "Any ideas who they were working for?"

He rubbed his chin. "Ah yes, Mr Nicholas De Ville and his gang. Still a bit foggy on that one. We don't think they were working for the Albanians. They'd have just locked the illegals back up if that was the case. The trafficking gang wouldn't have wanted them running all over the country with stolen silver. No, that had to be some attempt at a distraction."

"Have you got any other theories?"

He gave me a shrewd look. "There were a few other international salvage operations trying to get to that silver. I suspect one of them decided to try to snatch it from the warehouse when they'd been beaten to it on the seabed. And they either bribed De Ville to work with them – or he saw the opportunity and contacted them. They probably had a container ship waiting for the cargo somewhere on the coast this morning. We're trying to check out the nearest ports, but we aren't getting much help from him and his cronies at the moment. Maybe they'll crack nearer the time of the trial. It happens sometimes."

I nodded. That made sense. I doubted that a supposedly friendly foreign government would run a secret operation in the UK for the sake of £32 million. But another South African salvage enterprise would be a different thing.

"I've read all of your statements," continued the Chief Inspector as he continued to stroke Eddie. "And it's quite a story. I think, in the circumstances, and in the light of your assistance, we'll overlook your trespass into the tunnels. But no more underground seances, is that understood young lady?" Heloise nodded sheepishly. "And we're a bit baffled by that sudden cloud of steam and the tannoy working. Still, the machinery down there must be a bit temperamental by now, mustn't it? It's ancient. But it was one hell of a stroke of luck that you discovered the old tunnel to the canal. And full marks for effort and achievement on using it to get out and raise the alarm."

We looked at each other sheepishly but the policeman must have thought it was just modesty. We had quietly agreed amongst ourselves to exclude Gilbert's assistance from our witness statements.

The policeman gently urged Eddie to abandon his lap for the floor and rubbed both of his hands together in satisfaction. "Yes, all in all, a most satisfactory operation. Of course, the cards fell luckily for us. The tactical firearms units had been on an anti-terrorism exercise in Birmingham and so they were already on the road when we called for them. And the duty inspector you spoke to is a bright lad. He googled your name while you were on the phone to him and saw that you've got a bit of a track record. Still, it's all about how you play the hand that you're dealt isn't it?"

"Yes, it definitely is," said Heloise, and we all laughed.

"Well now, I must get going. Lots more to do. A police diver will retrieve your phones and clothes from the cave tomorrow. Thank you again. I'm sure the trial judge will have some nice words to say too. It'll be quite a story for the papers when it all gets out."

Nina looked at me. "Yes, I'm sure it will," she said with a smile.

The Chief Inspector paused with me before stepping off the boat and looked around him. "It's a nice spot to moor up, isn't it? It's full of history around here. They reckon King Charles walked or rode along the route of the canal when he was escaping after Worcester. It was a main thoroughfare then and Brindley just followed the contours of the road when he built the canal." He laughed to himself. "So, if you hear the sound of cavalry jangling in the night, it'll be 400-year-old ghosts!"

"I think I've had enough ghosts for the moment," I said.

He gave me a curious look, shook my hand, and disappeared into the dusk with his sergeant.

Back inside the boat, I pulled the half-full bottle of Black Grouse from its locker, poured generous measures into three glasses and added splashes of water. But before picking her glass up, Heloise dipped a hand into her multicoloured shoulder bag and put a bundle of £50 notes on a little side table. "There you go, refunded in full," she said. "I'm sorry it was such an ordeal, and that you didn't get to hear from Alan," she added to Nina.

"Oh no, that's not necessary," I said.

"I absolutely insist, and we won't remain friends if you don't take it," she said firmly.

"But what about the work you need to do on your boat?" asked Nina.

Heloise turned her amazing sapphire-coloured eyes on her. "To be honest, I don't need your money for that anymore. I've come into a bit of my own," she added mysteriously. We clinked glasses and treated the whisky with a moment of silent respect.

It was a cosy evening as the three of us chatted about the events of the night before and our future plans. At one point, our tongues loosened by alcohol, we tried to quiz Heloise about the moment when she wrote in the spilt water on the floor of the studio and showed us the entrance to the Devil's Den tunnel. However, she was at a loss to explain it.

"I suppose I was just taken over by Gilbert's spirit," was all she could say.

Nina and I would spend another week on the mooring and then move on northwards. Heloise was planning to have her boat lifted out of the canal and given a thorough overhaul.

Later, after our guest had gone, I dished up some cheese on toast, we finished the whisky and agreed on an early night after giving Eddie his last walk of the day. I was too tired for my book and my head hit the pillow with a grateful thud. But then I heard the swing door creak and I saw Nina's dim shape coming towards my bed. I went to sit up but felt her hand on my chest. It pushed me back into a prone position.

"I just wanted to say well done," she said quietly.

"You did pretty well yourself," I croaked.

Then she hooked a hand behind my head, and I felt her lips on mine. I tried to sit up again, but she pushed me back down for a second time.

"So - Amsterdam, here we come," she said in a more matter of fact tone.

"Sounds great," I said thickly.

"I wonder where Heloise got the money for her boat. I felt a bit guilty taking my £200 back."

"Oh, I wouldn't feel too bad," I said.

Nina detected something in my tone. "What d'you mean?"

"Well," I said. "Did you notice that throughout last night, climbing in and out of that air duct, working in the chain gang, bashing open the tunnel in the radio studio – one thing never left her side?"

Nina thought for a moment. "Her shoulder bag?"

"Yep." I reached up for my mobile phone on a bookshelf, brought it to life and pressed the calculator button. "And she still had it with her when she walked out of the tunnel."

"What are you saying?" asked Nina in the darkness.

"Let's see now, shall we. There were 2,364 silver ingots worth £32 million pounds in total. So, a quick division and, yes, if my maths is right, one single ingot is worth £13,536."

"The missing bar of silver!" exclaimed Nina.

"Yes, that should just cover the cost of a modest overhaul for Magic Meg."

We clinked our glasses and our laughter bubbled out of the boat and rippled along the inky black water until it lapped at the door of The Devil's Den.

AUTHOR'S NOTE

All of the characters and plot elements featured in Devil's Den are entirely fictional products of my imagination. However, as the frontispiece map indicates, the action is set on a real stretch of the Staffs & Worcs Canal which includes the small cave/boathouse of the title.

The history and geography of The Millionaire Tunnels in the book draws heavily on the real-life Drakelow Tunnels, which are located further to the south of Kinver. These have been renamed and relocated under the Millions nature reserve in the story, both for legal reasons and to make the plot work (by giving them crawling proximity to The Devil's Den).

The details of the excavation of the tunnel complex, their history as a wartime factory and a nuclear shelter, their popularity among paranormal groups and the existence of the museum are all factual. All else is fiction, although the 'hauntings', including the tannoy system breaking into life, the appearance of the underground mist and the tunnels' fearful impact on dogs have all been reported at Drakelow. It is up to the reader how much credence he or she chooses to give them.

The details of the salvage operation for the silver and the size and value of the haul are also true. The storage of the silver ingots in the tunnels, however, is complete fiction.

I would like to thank Alisha Adcock for her generous help with the tarot card reading scene and Deb Palin for gifting me a pack of cards. Thanks also to my friends Mike Mockett, Kate Hinchley and Ian and Fiona Wright for joining me on above and below ground research.

My grateful thanks are also due to beta readers David Birt (a fellow border terrier owner), Stuart Makemson (a boater) and to Al Rayner for additional historical material. I am indebted, once again, to Michael Pearson of Pearson's Canal Companions and his daughter Tamar for the frontispiece map and to boater, Alan Buckle of Star Crafts for the cover picture (design by Orphans Publishing).

Finally, thanks once again to my wife Helen who also joined me on research forays around Kinver with Eddie and who never fails to give me encouragement, advice and support.

A donation will be made to Drakelow Tunnels Museum from the sales of this book in recognition of the volunteers' preservation and education work, and as a token of respect for the people who died during the construction of the tunnel complex.

ABOUT THE AUTHOR

Andy Griffee

Andy Griffee is a former BBC journalist and senior manager who swapped factual writing for fiction five years ago. He chose to set his books on canals and rivers so that his hero, Jack Johnson, could move around the country and because of their inherent danger. He also believes the tensions between different groups using the waterways make them a great setting for his 'Canal Noir' tiller-thrillers. Andy lives in Worcestershire with his wife and two Border terriers (one of whom is called Eddie). When he isn't writing, he rears rare breed pigs, struggles to keep a 1964 Triumph Spitfire on the road and enjoys going on narrowboat trips which inspire new plot twists as the towpath rolls past.

BOOKS BY THIS AUTHOR

Canal Pushers

Jack Johnson, a divorced and unemployed journalist is seeking a fresh start and decides to try living in a narrowboat. But he's a duffer with the sixty-four-foot boat until he meets the enigmatic Nina Wilde on the towpath and she comes to his rescue. A chance meeting with a homeless young man and his dog sets off a sequence of events that leads to a perilous chase across the Midlands canal network. Can Jack and Nina escape from a media manhunt, a drugs gang and the mysterious Canal Pusher with their lives?

River Rats

Jack moves on and moors up in the refined Georgian splendour of Bath where he picks up shifts on a local newspaper. If only Nina would move onto his boat, Jumping Jack Flash, he'd be a happy man. A prominent heritage campaigner is drowned and Jack finds himself pulled into the investigation at the same time as he befriends a small boating community on the River Avon. But greedy property developers want to get rid of the cluster of boats moored alongside their new luxury housing scheme. A gripping tale of crime, corruption and intrigue unfurls on the West Country's waterways.

Oxford Blues

It's winter in Oxford and Jack has moved on to the River Isis in pursuit of Nina, whose niece is studying at the university. He's hoping their relationship will get a kick-start in the city of dreaming spires. But instead, it gets a kick in the teeth when Nina befriends Caleb Hopper, a young American member of the university's rowing team. The body of Caleb's girlfriend has been dragged up from Iffley Lock by magnet fishermen and Jack is soon embroiled in a tale of drowned love and dirty business.

Printed in Great Britain
by Amazon